Sleeping Fires

George Gissing

SLEEPING FIRES

George Gissing

University of Nebraska Press
Lincoln and London

First published in 1895 by T. Fisher Unwin

Manufactured in the United States of America

First Bison Book printing: December 1983

Most recent printing indicated by the first digit below:

1   2   3   4   5   6   7   8   9   10

Library of Congress Cataloging in Publication Data

Gissing, George, 1857–1903.

   Sleeping fires.

   Reprint. Originally published: London : T. Fisher
Unwin, 1895. (The Autonym library)

   I. Title.

PR4716.S6 1983   823'.8   83-12402

ISBN 0-8032-7011-9 (pbk.)

HE rain was over. As he sat reading Langley saw the page illumined with a flood of sunshine, which warmed his face and hand. For a few minutes he read on, then closed his Aristophanes with a laugh—faint echo of the laughter of more than two thousand years ago.

He had passed the winter at Athens, occupying rooms, chosen for the prospects they commanded, in a hotel unknown to his touring countrymen, where the waiters had no English, and only a smattering of French or Italian. No economic necessity constrained him. Within sight of the Acropolis he did not care to be constantly reminded of Piccadilly or the Boulevard—that was all. He consumed *pilafi* and meats generously enriched with the native oil, drank resinated wine, talked such Greek as Heaven permitted. At two and forty, whether by choice or pressure of circumstance, a man may be doing worse.

The cup and plate of his early breakfast were still on the table, with volumes many, in many languages, heaped about them. Langley looked at his watch, rose with deliberation, stretched himself, and walked to the window. Hence, at a southern angle, he saw the Parthenon, honey-coloured against a violet sky, and at the opposite limit of his view the peak of Lycabettus; between and beyond, through

the pellucid air which at once reveals and softens its barren rugged-
ness, Hymettus basking in the light of spring. He could not grow
weary of such a scene, which he had watched through changes
innumerable of magic gleam and shade since the sunsets of autumn
fired it with solemn splendour; but his gaze this morning was directed
merely by habit. With the laugh he had forgotten Aristophanes, and
now, as his features told, was possessed with thought of some modern, some personal interest, a care, it seemed, and perchance that one,
woven into the fabric of his life, which accounted for deep lines on a
face otherwise expressing the contentment of manhood in its prime.

A second time he consulted his watch—perhaps because he had no
appointment, nor any call whatever upon his time. Then he left the
room, crossed a corridor, and entered his bedchamber to make ready
for going forth. Thus equipped he presented a recognisable type of
English gentleman, without eccentricity of garb, without originality,
clad for ease and for the southern climate, but obviously by a London
tailor. Ever so slight a bend of shoulders indicated the bookman, but
he walked, even in sauntering, with free, firm step, and looked about
him like a man of this world. The face was pleasant to encounter,
features handsome and genial, moustache and beard, in hue something like the foliage of a copper-beech, peculiarly well trimmed. At a
little distance one judged him on the active side of forty. His lineaments provoked another estimate, but with no painful sense of disillu-
sion.

Careless of direction, he strolled to the public market—the Bazaar,
as it is called—where, as in the Athens of old, men, not women, were
engaged in marketing, and where fish seemed a commodity no less
important than when it nourished the sovereign Demos. Thence, by
the Street of Athena, head bent in thought, to the street of Hermes,
where he loitered as if in uncertainty, indifference leading him at
length to the broad sunshine of that dusty, desolate spot where stands
the Temple of Theseus. So nearly perfect that it can scarce be called a
ruin, there, on the ragged fringe of modern Athens, hard by the station

of the Piræus Railway, its marble majesty consecrates the ravaged soil. A sanctuary still, so old, so wondrous in its isolation, that all the life of to-day around it seems a futility and an impertinence.

Looking dreamily before him, Langley saw a man who drew near—a man with a book under one arm, an umbrella under the other, and an open volume in his hands—a tourist, of course, and probably an Englishman, for his garb was such as no native of a civilised country would exhibit among his own people. His eccentric straw hat, with a domed crown and an immense brim, shadowed a long, thin visage disguised with blue spectacles. A grey Norfolk jacket moulded itself to his meagre form; below were flannel trousers, very baggy at the knees, and a pair of sand-shoes. This individual, absorbed in study of the book he held open, moved forward with a slow, stumbling gait. He was arrested at length, and all but overthrown, by coming in contact with the sword-pointed leaf of a great agave. Langley, now close at hand, barely refrained from laughter. He had averted his eyes, when, with no little astonishment, he heard himself called by name. The stranger—for Langley tried in vain to recognise him—hurried forward with a hand of greeting.

"Don't you remember me?—Worboys."

"Of course! In another moment your voice would have declared you to me. I seemed to hear some one calling from an immense distance—knew I ought to know the voice——"

They shook hands cordially.

"Good heavens, Langley! To think that we should meet in the Kerameikos! You know that we are in the Kerameikos? I've got Pausanias here, but it really is so extremely difficult to identify the sites——"

Fifteen years had elapsed since their last meeting; but Worboys, oblivious of the trifle, plunged forthwith into a laborious statement of his topographic and archæologic perplexities. He talked just as at Cambridge, where his ponderous pedantry had been wont to excite Langley's amusement, at the same time that the sterling qualities of

the man attracted his regard. Anything but brilliantly endowed, Worboys, by dint of plodding, achieved academic repute, got his fel-
lowship, and pursued a career of erudition. He was known to schools
and colleges by his exhaustive editing of the "Cyropædia." Langley,
led by fate into other paths, gradually lost sight of his entertaining
friend. That their acquaintance should be renewed "in the .Ker-
ameikos" was appropriate enough, and Langley's mood prepared him
to welcome the incident.

"Are you here alone?" he asked, when civility allowed him to
wave Pausanias aside.

"No; I am bear-leading. Last autumn, I regret to say, I had a rather
serious illness, and travel was recommended. It happened at the same
time that Lord Henry Strands—I was his young brother's tutor, by the
by—spoke to me of a lady who wished to find a travelling companion
for a young fellow, a ward of hers. I somewhat doubted my suitabil-
ity—the conditions of the case were peculiar—but after an interview
with Lady Revill——"

The listener's half-absent smile changed of a sudden to a look of
surprise and close attention.

"—I gave my assent. He's a lad of eighteen without parents to look
after him, and really a difficult subject. I much fear that he finds my
companionship wearisome; at all events, he gets out of my way as
often as he can. Louis Reed is his name. I'm afraid he has caused his
guardian a great deal of anxiety. And Lady Revill—such an admirable person, I really can't tell you how I admire and respect her—she
regards him quite as her son."

"Lady Revill has no child of her own, I believe?" said Langley.

"No. You are acquainted with her?"

"I knew her before her marriage."

"Indeed! What a delightful coincidence! I can't tell you how she
impresses me. Of course I am not altogether unaccustomed to the
society of such people, but Lady Revill—I really regard her as the
very best type of aristocratic woman, I do indeed. She must have been
most interesting in her youth."

"Do you think of her as old?" Langley asked, with a grave smile.

"Oh, not exactly old—oh, dear no! I imagine that her age—well, I never gave the matter a thought."

"Does she seem——?" Langley hesitated, dropping his look. "Should you say that her life has been a pleasant one?"

"Oh, undoubtedly! Well, that is to say, we must remember that she has suffered a sad loss. I believe Sir Thomas Revill was a most admirable man."

"She speaks of him?"

"Not to me. But I have heard from others. Not a distinguished man, of course; silent, as a member of Parliament, I believe, but admirable in all private relations. To be sure, I have only heard of him casually. You knew him?"

"By repute. I should say you are quite right about him. And this boy gives you a good deal of trouble?"

"No, no!" Worboys exclaimed hurriedly. "I didn't wish to convey that impression. To begin with, one can hardly call him a boy. No, he is singularly mature for his age. And yet I don't mean mature; on the contrary, he abounds in youthful follies. I don't wish to convey an impression—really it's very difficult to describe him. But of course you will come and have lunch with us, Langley? He'll be at the hotel by one o'clock, no doubt. I left him writing letters—he's always writing letters. Really, I am tempted to imagine some—but he doesn't confide in me, and I seldom allow myself to talk of anything but serious subjects."

They were moving in the townward direction. Langley, divided between his own thoughts and attention to what his companion was saying, walked with eyes on the ground.

"And what have you been doing all these years?" Worboys inquired. "Strange how completely we have drifted apart. I knew you on the instant. You have changed wonderfully little. And how pleasant it is to hear your voice again! Life is so short; friends ought not to lose sight of each other. *Soles occidere et redire possunt*—you know."

The other gave a brief and good-humoured account of himself.

"And you have lived here alone all the winter," said Worboys. "Not like you; you were so sociable; the life and soul of our old symposia—though I don't know that I ought to say *our,* for I seldom found time to join in such relaxations. A pity; I regret it. The illness of last autumn made me all at once an old man. And no doubt that's why Louis finds me so unsympathetic. Though I like him; yes, I really like him. Don't imagine that he is illiterate. He'll make a notable man, if he lives. Yes, I regret to say that his health leaves much to be desired. In Italy he had a troublesome fever—not grave, but difficult to shake off. He lives at such high pressure; perpetual fever of the mind. Our project was to spend a whole twelve-month abroad. We ought not to have reached Athens till the autumn of this year; yet here we are. Louis can't stay in any place more than a week or so, and to resist him is really dangerous—I mean for his health. Lady Revill allows me complete discretion, but it's really Louis who directs our travel. I wanted to devote at least a month to the antiquities at Rome. There are several questions I should like to have settled for myself. For instance——"

He went off into Roman archæology, and his companion, excused from listening, walked in reverie. Thus they ascended the long street of Hermes, which brought them to the Place of the Constitution, and in view of Mr. Worboys' hotel, the approved resort which Langley had taken trouble to avoid. As they drew near to the entrance, a young man, walking briskly, approached from the opposite quarter, and of a sudden Worboys exclaimed:

"Ha! here comes our young friend."

II

OUIS, let me introduce you to a very old friend of mine, Mr. Langley. We were contemporaries at Cambridge, and after many years we meet unexpectedly in the Kerameikos!''

The young man stepped forward with peculiarly frank and pleasant address. It was evident at a glance that his physique would support no serious strain; he had a very light and graceful figure, with narrow shoulders, small hands and feet, and a head which for beauty and poise would not have misbecome the youthful Hermes. Grotesque indeed was the aspect of his blue-spectacled tutor standing side by side with Louis. On the other hand, when he and Langley came together, a certain natural harmony appeared in the two figures; it might even have been observed that their faces offered a mutual resemblance, sufficient to excuse a stranger for supposing them akin. Louis, though only a gold down appeared upon his chin, and the mere suggestion of a moustache on his lip, looked older than he was by two or three years; perhaps the result of that slight frown, a fixed but not unamiable characteristic of his physiognomy, which was noticeable also on Langley's visage. The elder man bearing his age so lightly, they might have been taken for brothers.

''I have been to the Cemetery,'' was Louis's first remark. ''Do you know it, Mr. Langley? The monuments are nearly as hideous as those at Naples. There's a marble life-sized medallion of a man in his habit as he lived, and, by Jove, if they haven't gilded the studs in his shirt-front!''

"How interesting!'' exclaimed the tutor. "The sculptors of the great age were just as realistic.''

"With a difference,'' Langley interposed.

"And something else that will delight you, Mr. Worboys,'' the youth continued. "There's a public notice, painted on a board, in continuous lettering, without spaces—just like the *Codices*!''

His emphasis on the last word evidently had humorous reference to Mr. Worboys' habits of speech. Langley smiled, but Worboys was delighted.

"But they stick a skull and crossbones on their tombs,'' pursued Louis. "That's hideously degenerate. Your ancient friends, Mr. Worboys, knew better how to deal with death.''

To Langley's ears this remark had an unexpectedness which made him regard the speaker more closely. Louis had something more in him than youthful vivacity and sprightliness; his soft-glancing eyes could look below the surface of things.

"You observe, Langley,'' said the tutor, "that he speaks of *my* ancient friends. Louis is a terribly modern young man. I can't get him to care much about the classical civilisations. The idea of his running off to see a new cemetery, when he hasn't yet seen the Theseion! And that reminds me, Langley; I am strongly tempted to believe with some of the Germans that the Theseion isn't a temple of Theseus at all. I'll show you my reasons.''

He did so, with *Ausführlichkeit* and *Gründlichkeit,* as they ascended the steps of the hotel. Langley, the while, continued observant of Louis Reed, with whom, presently, he was able to converse at his ease; for Worboys recognized that the costume in which it delighted him to roam among ruins would be inappropriate at the luncheon-table. Louis, when the waiter in the vestibule had dusted him from head to heel—a necessary service performed for all who entered—

needed to make no change of dress; he wore the clothing which would have suited him on a warm spring day in England, and the minutiæ of his attire denoted a quiet taste, a sense of social propriety, agreeable to Langley's eye. They had no difficulty in exchanging reflections on things Continental. Louis talked with animation, yet with deference. It was easy to perceive his pleasure in finding an acquaintance more sympathetic than the erudite but hidebound Worboys.

When all three sat down to the meal, Worboys drew attention to the wine that was put before him, Côtes de Parnès, with the brand of "Solon and Co."

"We cannot drink the wine of the gods," he observed with a chuckle, "but here is the next best thing—the wine of the philosophers."

Louis averted his face. It was the fifth day since their arrival at Athens, and his tutor had indulged in this joke at least once daily.

"By the by, Langley, where are you staying?"

Langley named the hotel, and briefly described it.

"How interesting! Yes, that's much better."

"I should think so!" exclaimed Louis. "Why shouldn't we go there, Mr. Worboys? Living like this, what can we get to know of the life of the country? That's what I care about, Mr. Langley. I want to see how the people live nowadays. It matters very little what they did ages ago. It seems to me that life isn't long enough to live in the past as well as in the present."

"Yet you concern yourself a great deal with the future, my dear boy," remarked Worboys.

"Yes; I can't help that. Isn't the future growing in us? And surely it's a duty to——"

Either incapacity to express himself, or a modest self-restraint, caused him to break off and bend over his plate. For some minutes after this he kept silence, whilst Mr. Worboys pleaded, in set phrase, for the study of the classics and all that appertained thereto. Langley observed that the young man ate delicately and sparingly, but that he was by no means so moderate in his use of the philosophic beverage. Louis drank glass after glass of undiluted wine, a practice which his tutor's classic sympathies ought surely to have disapproved. But possibly Mr. Worboys, even without his coloured spectacles, had not become aware of it.

They repaired to the smoking room, where Louis lit a cigarette. The wine had not made him talkative; rather it seemed to lull his vivacious temper, to wrap him in meditation or day-dream. He lay back and watched the curling of the smoke; on his emotional lips a smile of gentle melancholy, his eyes wide and luminous in mental vision. When he had sat thus for a few minutes, he was approached by a waiter, who handed him two letters. Instantly his countenance flashed into vivid life; having glanced at the writing on the envelopes, he held them with a tight grasp; and very shortly, seeing that his friends were conversing, he walked from the room.

"There now," remarked Worboys. "He's been wild with impatience for letters. One of them, no doubt, is from Lady Revill, but it isn't *that* he was waiting for. Do you know a certain Mrs. Tresilian?"

"What—*the* Mrs. Tresilian?"

"Really, I never heard the name till Louis spoke of her. Is she distinguished? A lady of so-called advanced opinions."

"Yes, yes; the Mrs. Tresilian of public fame, no doubt," said Langley, with interest. "I don't know her personally. Is she a friend of his?"

"My dear Langley, it sounds very absurd, but I'm afraid the poor boy has quite lost his head about her. And I suspect—I only *suspect*—that Lady Reville wished to remove him beyond the sphere of her malign influence. She spoke to me of 'unfortunate influences' in his life, but mentioned no name. Who is this lady? What is her age?"

"I know very little of her, except that she addresses meetings on political and humanitarian subjects. A woman with a head, I believe, and rather eloquent. Her age? Oh, five and thirty, perhaps, to judge from her portraits. Handsome, undeniably. How can he have got into her circle?"

"I have no idea," Worboys replied, with a gesture of helplessness. "I know nothing of that sphere."

"And they correspond?"

"I am convinced they do; though Louis has never said so. I surmise it from his talk in—in moments of unusual expansiveness. And imagine how it must distress such a person as Lady Revill!"

Langley mused before he spoke again.

"You mean that she fears for his—or the lady's—morals?"

"Oh, dear me, I didn't mean that! But the effects on a young, excitable nature of such principles as Mrs. Tresilian appears to hold! Perhaps you are not aware of the strong conservatism of Lady Revill's mind?"

"I see," faltered the other. "She seriously desires to guard him from 'advanced opinion'?"

"Most seriously. I have told you that she has almost a maternal affection for the boy. How it must shock her to see him going off into those wild speculations—seeking to undermine all she reverences!"

"Is he such a revolutionist?" Langley asked, with a smile.

"Well, I have sometimes thought him a sort of Shelley," ventured the tutor, with amusing diffidence. "Though I don't know that he writes verses. However, you see the points of similarity? A strange youth, altogether. As I said, I can't help liking him. I daresay he'll outgrow his follies.'

Langley smoked and was silent. The other, thinking the subject dismissed, uttered a remark tending to matters archaic; but Langley disregarded it and spoke again.

"What's his origin—do you know?"

"Really, I don't. He never speaks of it—Lady Revill only said that he was an orphan, and her ward."

"Where has he been educated?"

"Private tutors, and private schools. Of course Lady Revill wishes him to pass to a University, but it seems he is set against it. He has some extraordinary idea that he is old enough, and educated sufficiently, to begin the serious business of life; though I don't gather what he means exactly by that. I conceive that Mrs. Tresilian is responsible for such vagaries. He appears to reprobate the thought of being connected with the aristocracy—part of his Shelleyism, of course. I almost believe that he would like to take some active part in democratic politics."

"H'm—the type is familiar," murmured Langley. "Nothing very abnormal about him, I daresay. And it occurred to Lady Revill that your companionship might abate these ecstasies?"

"That," Worboys replied, with modesty, "appears to have been her view. A student who has given some proof of solid attainment might naturally seem——"

"To be sure," interposed the other, suavely. "But our young friend seems cut out for rather obstinate independence."

"I really fear so." And Mr. Worboys shook his sage head.

At this moment Louis re-entered the room. He had a flushed face, and an air of exaltation. Stepping rapidly up to the two men, he threw himself upon a chair beside them, and said with a boyish laugh:

"Well, Mr. Worboys, I'm quite ready for the Theseion or the Kerameikos, or anything you like to propose. But when are we going to Salamis—and to Marathon—and to climb Pentelikon? I should really like to see Marathon. And Thermopylæ better still. Of course we must get to Thermopylæ."

This led to a discussion with Langley of facilities for travel in the remoter parts of Greece. It ended in their all strolling out together, and having a drive to Phaleron, on the white dusty road which is the fashionable course for carriages and equestrians at Athens. Worboys talked about the "Long Walls"; Louis Reed was in a sportive spirit, and found mirth in everything. Their companion said little, but listened good-naturedly and smiled. Once, too, when his eyes had been fixed for a moment on the boy's bright countenance, he seemed to sigh.

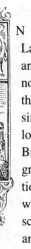

III

I N the view of most of his acquaintances, Edmund Langley's life seemed to have followed a very smooth and ordinary course. There was no break of continuity, no sudden change in himself or his circumstances, in the retrospect of two and twenty years: that is to say, since he began to disappoint the friends who had looked to him for a brilliant career at Cambridge. Brilliant, in a manner, it was; in his undergraduate group he shone as a leading light, and later his reputation as a man of clever and imposing talk, held good with those who regretted his failure in the contests of scholarship. He left the University with a mere degree, and went to London to read law.

It was very leisurely reading, for no necessity spurred him on. His ambitions at that time were political, and he enjoyed a private income which allowed him to think of Parliament; personally devoted to a liberal culture, he was prepared to take the popular-progressive side, and to accept with genial humour those articles of the popular creed which he no longer held with his early enthusiasm. But nothing came of it. When, in his twenty-sixth year, an opportunity of candidature offered itself, he declined for rather vague reasons, and soon after it became known that he was to accompany on extensive travels a young nobleman, who had been his contemporary at Cambridge. Six months after their departure from England, the luckless Peer suffered a perilous accident, which lamed him for life. They returned, and Langley, for some fifteen years, remained with his friend as private secretary. In that capacity he had very little to do, but the life was agreeable; he found satisfaction in the society of a liberal-minded circle, learned to smile at the projects of his early manhood, and soothed his leisure with studies utterly remote from any popular or progressive programme. The nobleman's death enriched him with a legacy of which he stood in no need whatever, and murmuring to himself, "To him that hath shall be given," he wandered off to spend a year or two abroad.

Beneath this placid flow of existence lay hidden a sorrow of which he spoke to no one. The occasion of it was far behind him, in the years of turbulent youth; for a long time it had troubled him little, and only when his spirits invited care; but these latter months of solitude tended to revive the old distress, with new features attributable to the stage of life that he had reached. He knew not whether to be glad or sorry, when a casual meeting at Athens brought vividly before his mind the bygone things he had so long tried to forget.

After the drive with Worboys and Louis Reed, he returned to his hotel in a mood of melancholy. The evening, usually a pleasant enough time over his books, dragged with something worse than tedium; and the night that followed was such as he had not known for many years. Out of the darkness, a tormenting memory evoked two faces; the one pale and blurred, refusing distinct presentment, even to the obstinate efforts which, in spite of himself, he repeated hour after hour; the other so distinct, so living, that at moments it thrilled him as with a touch of the supernatural—a light on the features, a play of expression, all but a voice from the moving lips. Faces of character much unlike, though both female, and both young. The one which haunted him elusively had but a superficial charm: no depth in the smiling eyes, no intellectual beauty on the brows; the moment's fancy of sensual youth; powerless to subdue, to retain. The other, clear upon the gloom, spoke a finer womanhood, so much more nobly endowed in qualities of flesh and spirit that its beauty seemed to scorn comparison. Animation, self-command, the dignity of breeding and intelligence, lighted its lineaments. It was the woman whom a man in his maturity desires unashamed.

In these visions of the troubled night he saw also a large house, old and pleasant to the eye, which stood beyond the limits of a manufacturing town, planted about with fair trees, and walled from the frequented highway. He heard a soft roll of carriage wheels on the drive, the sound of cheery voices beneath the portico; he felt the languid, scented air of an old-time garden, where fruits hung ripe. And in the garden walked Agnes Forrest, youngest of the children of the house, but already in her twenty-first year. Her father was no man of yesterday's uprising, but the son and grandson of substantial merchants; he sat among his family and his guests, a reverend potentate.

The suggestion of her name did not well accord with Agnes' character. Had humility been her distinguishing virture, Langley would never have made her his ideal of womanhood. He knew her strong of will, and found her opinions frequently at variance with his own; all the more delightful to perceive his influence in the directing of her mind. She was no great student, and took her full share in the active pleasures of life; rode as well as she danced; seemed to have admirable judgment in dress; enjoyed society, and liked to shine in it. Her ridicule of sentimentalities by no means discouraged the lover; it suited his taste, and could throw no doubt upon the capacity for strong feeling which he had often noted in her. The general conservatism of her thought was far from distasteful to him, smile as he might at some of its manifestations; she never opposed reason with mere feminine prejudice, and Langley was disposed to regard woman as the natural safeguard of traditions that have an abiding value. She was not a girl to be lightly wooed, and won as a matter of course. Her beauty and her brilliant social qualities cost him many an anxious hour, even when he believed himself gently encouraged. She did not conceal her ambitions; happily, he felt that she credited him with abilities of the conquering kind.

The old-time garden, and two who walked there, with long silences between the words that still disguised their deeper meaning. Langley knew himself peculiarly welcome to the parents, and felt a reasonable assurance that Agnes wished him to speak. On this same day, as it chanced, Sir Thomas Revill, the borough member, a widower of middle age, was one of the guests. Mr. Forrest seemed less cordial to the baronet than to the friend of lower rank. But Langley let the day pass, for a scruple restrained his tongue. After a night when temptation had all but vanquished conscience, he sought a private interview with Agnes' father.

"Mr. Forrest," he began frankly, yet with diffidence, "you cannot but see that I love your daughter, and that I wish to ask her if she will be my wife."

"I have suspected it, my dear Langley," was the old man's reply, as he smiled with satisfaction.

"I dare not speak to her until I have told you something, which perhaps you will think ought to have forbidden me to approach Miss Forrest at all.—Three years ago, in London, I formed a connection which resulted in my becoming the father of a child. The mother subsequently married, and left England, taking this child with her— her own desire, and with the consent of her husband. I could not oppose it; perhaps I hardly felt any desire to do so, though I need not say that mother and child both had a claim upon me which I never dreamt of disputing. Her place in life was below my own, and she married a man of her own class. When she last took leave of me—we had lived apart for more than a year—I told her that, if circumstances ever made it necessary, she was to look to me again for aid, and that, if ever she desired it, I would bring up the child in every way as my own—short of public acknowledgment. She went to South Africa, and I have since heard nothing. But there is still the possibility that I may be called upon to keep my word. This I am obliged to tell you. I cannot speak of it to Miss Forrest."

He paused with eyes cast down, and Mr. Forrest kept a short silence.

"An unpleasant business, Langley," the old man remarked at length, in a perplexed, but not a severe voice. "Of course you are right to speak of it. A very awkward matter."

He mused again, then began to interrogate. Langley answered with all frankness. He was not responsible for the girl's lapse from virtue; that must be laid to the account of the man who at length married her. In every respect, save for this trouble of conscience, he was honourably free.

"The deuce of it is," exclaimed Mr. Forrest, at last, "that women have a way of their own of regarding this sort of thing. For my own part—well, a young man is a young man. You were three and twenty. I can understand and excuse. But women——"

It did not occur to him to ask who the girl was, and on this point Langley offered no information beyond what he had said of her social position.

"I know quite well, Langley, that this, as it regards yourself, forms no presumption whatever against your making Agnes a good husband, if you married her. Your self-respect won't allow you to urge assurances of that; I know it all the same, because I have a pretty fair knowledge of you. But women think differently. There's nothing for it, I fear: I must talk with my wife about it."

Langley bowed to the decision he had foreseen. He went away with misery in his heart, cursing the honesty that had made him speak. Mr. Forrest's liberality of view might, only too probably, be explained by his certainty that Agnes' mother would never consent to the proposed marriage. "Should I myself give my daughter to a man who came with such a story?"

A day passed, and again he was closeted with the old man.

"Langley, my wife won't hear of this being mentioned to Agnes."

Oh, cursed folly! And it seemed, now, such an easy thing to have kept silence.

"It's my own fault. I ought never to have dared——"

"Remember, Langley, how very recently these things have happened."

"I know—I see all the folly, and worse, that I have been guilty of. Pardon it, if you can, Mr. Forrest, to one who is for the first time in love—and with Agnes."

Ten minutes, and all was over. Langley turned from the house, thinking to see its occupants no more.

But to the relief of misery came common-sense. What right had he thus to turn his back on Agnes without a word of explanation? His mysterious behaviour could not but result in confidences of some kind between Agnes and her parents. They, worthy people, assuredly would spare him; but, short of telling the truth, how could they avoid misrepresentation which in Agnes' mind must have all the effect of calumny? Impossible to let the matter end thus. He wrote to Mr. Forrest, and urged, with all respect, his claim to be judged by Agnes herself. Was she yet one and twenty? In any case she had attained responsible womanhood. He begged that this point might receive consideration.

"We were obliged to speak to Agnes," replied the father. "We have told her that something has happened which unexpectedly makes it impossible for you to think of marriage. This was all. I fear you have no choice but to preserve absolute silence. Agnes is just of age, but her mother and I feel very strongly that, out of regard for her happiness, you ought to think of her no more. Our friends, of course, shall never surmise anything disagreeable from our manner when you are spoken of. At the worst it will be imagined that Agnes has declined to marry you."

Regard for his old friends kept Langley silent for a week; then his passion overcame him. He wrote two letters—one to Agnes, simply offering marriage; the other to Mr. Forrest, saying what he had done, asserting his right, and begging that Agnes might be told the plain facts of the case before she answered him. The next day brought Mr. Forrest's reply, a few coldly civil lines, stating that Agnes had been informed of everything. Another day, and Agnes herself wrote, just as briefly—a courteous refusal.

Then Langley left England with his friend the nobleman. He had battled through amorous despair, but the disaster seemed to drain his life of hope and purpose; succumbing to fatality, he must make the best of sunless years.

A few months of travel dispelled this unnatural gloom. He began to foster the thought that Agnes' parents were both aged; it could not be expected that either would be alive ten years hence, and half that period might see both removed. If Agnes cared much for him, she would wait on the future. If he had been mistaken, and her heart were not gravely wounded, she would make proof of liberty by marrying another man. In which case——

Langley knew not how securely he had come to count upon Miss Forrest's fidelity, until one day the news reached him that she was Miss Forrest no longer. Agnes had married the middle-aged member of Parliament, and henceforth must be thought of as Lady Revill. That chapter of life, whether or not the doom of his existence, was finally closed. She had waited barely a twelvemonth, so that, in all likelihood, his timid lovemaking had but feebly impressed her. Another twelvemonth, and Mr. Forrest was dead; two years later Agnes' mother followed him. Oh, the folly of it all! The imbecile hesitation where common-sense pointed his path! She liked him well enough to marry him, and probably her life, as well as his own, must miss its consummation because he had played the pedant in morals.

This regret had long lost its poignancy, though it imparted a sober tinge to the epicureanism whereby Langley thought to direct his otherwise purposeless life. But the course of years shaped into conscious sorrow that loss which, as a young man, he had hardly regarded as a loss at all. He grew to an understanding of the wantonness with which he had acted in so lightly abandoning his child. Whilst the petty casuistry of his relations with Agnes Forrest was capable of compelling him into perverse heroism, he had committed what now seemed to

him a much graver recklessness—perhaps, indeed, a crime—with
but the faintest twinge of conscience. His child, his son, would now be
grown up—a young man, about the same age as Louis Reed; and in
such companionship how different would the world appear to him! In
love with Agnes, he had been glad to rid himself of a troublesome and
dangerous responsibility. For the mother—and this fact he had withheld in his confession—belonged to the town in which the Forrests
were practically resident, and where he had other friends; a coincidence unknown to him when he made her acquaintance in London.
Rescued from the evil of sense only to be rapt aloft by romantic
passion, what thought had he of the duties and the reward of paternity?
Now, a sobered and somewhat lonely man, he saw the result of his
hasty act in a very different light. Perchance the boy was dead; if
living, better perchance that he should have died. What future could
be hoped for him, delivered into such hands?

For the disregard of duty conscience offered excuse. His relations
with the girl had worn no semblance of conjugality; they never lived
together; he had seen the child but once or twice; every obligation
imposed by the worldly code of honour he had abundantly discharged.
The girl, moreover, had not loved him; he found her (though ignorant
of the circumstances till long afterwards) on the brink of hopeless
degradation, the result of her having been forsaken by the man for
whom she strayed, and whom she subsequently married. As far as *she*
was concerned he might reasonably be at rest, for in all probability his
conduct saved her from the abyss. But such reasoning did not help him
to forget that he had had a son, and that he had wantonly made himself
childless. It were well if the child did not at this moment think with
bitterness of an unknown parent, or, thinking not at all, live basely
amid base companions.

He had never sought for tidings of them; it was possible, and merely
possible, that inquiries in the town he never revisited might have had
results. But if the child's mother had wished to communicate with him
she could always have done so; that was provided for at their parting.

It might be that neither she nor the boy had ever needed him; the man she married, a petty traveller in commerce, perhaps behaved well to them in the new country; that the girl was permitted to take her child seemed in her husband's favour. For her, too, did it not speak well that she would not forsake the little one? A weak, silly girl, but not without good traits; he remembered her, though dimly, with kindness — nay, with a certain respect. After all——

Well, it was the sight of Louis Reed that had turned him to melancholy musing. A son of that age, a handsome intelligent lad, overflowing with the zeal and the zest of life; with such a one at his side how lightly and joyously would he walk among these ruins of the old world! What flow of talk! What happiness of silent sympathy!

So passed the night.

IV

HE window of Langley's bedroom opened on to a balcony, pleasant to him in early morning for the air and the view. Over the straggling outskirts of Athens he looked upon the plain, or broad valley, where Cephisus, with scant and precious flow, draws seaward through grey-green olive gardens, down from Acharnæ of the poet, past the bare hillock which is called Colonus, to the blue Phaleric bay. His eye loved to follow a far-winding track, mile after mile, away to the slope of Aigaleos, where the white road vanished in a ravine; for this was the Sacred Way, pursued of old by the procession of the Mysteries from Athens to Eleusis.

Here, on a morning when earth and sky were mated in unutterable calm and loveliness, he stood dreaming with unquiet heart. "They lived their life, enjoyed to the uttermost the golden day that was granted them. And I, whose day is passing, can only try to forget myself in the tale of their vanished glory. Is it too late? Are the hopes and energies of life for ever withdrawn?"

A voice called to him from below; he looked down into the street and saw Louis waving a friendly hand.

"Do you feel disposed to climb Lycabettus?" shouted the young man.

"Gladly! With you in a moment."

It was ten days since their first meeting, and in the meanwhile they had been much together; occasionally without Worboys, whose archæologic zeal delighted in solitude. Langley found an increasing pleasure in Louis' society, evinced by the readiness with which he hastened forth to meet him. This companionship revived in him some of the fervours of youth; even—strange as it seemed to him—turned his mind to some of the old ambitions. Yet he tried to subdue the symptoms of febrile temperament which overcame Louis in sympathetic conversation; good-humouredly, almost affectionately, he struck the note of disillusioned age; and it gratified him to see how the young man put restraint upon himself to listen patiently and answer with respect. Already, in a measure, he was succeeding where Worboys had so signally failed.

At a vigorous pace they breasted the hillside, turning often to gaze at the dazzling whiteness of Athens below them, and at the wondrous panorama spreading around as they ascended. On reaching the quarries Louis pointed with indignation to the girls and women who toiled at breaking up stone.

"That's the kind of thing that makes me detest these countries!"

"What about cotton-mills and match factories?" said Langley. "It's better breaking stone on Lycabettus."

"Well, both are alike damnable. Women shouldn't work in such ways at all."

"Doesn't your friend Mrs. Tresilian prefer it to idle dependence upon men?"

"Perhaps so," Louis replied, with the brightness of countenance which always accompanied a thought of Mrs. Tresilian. "But that's only for the present, until society can be civilised. Talking of that reminds me of something I wanted to ask you. Wouldn't it be possible for me to get—some day—an inspectorship of factories? How are they appointed?"

"Good heavens! This is your latest inspiration?"

"Please don't be contemptuous, Mr. Langley. I see no reason why I shouldn't be able to qualify myself. It's the kind of thing that would suit me exactly."

"Oh, admirably! Ordained from eternity, in the fitness of things! Pray, has Mrs. Tresilian suggested it?"

"No. But she certainly would approve it. The difficulty is to find an employment in which I can be of some use to the world. I hate the idea of the professions and the businesses, with nothing before me but money-making. And I've tried incessantly to think of something respectable—you know what I mean by that—which I could hope to do effectually. It would delight me to get an inspectorship of factories and workshops. The satisfaction of coming down on brutes who break the laws—every kind of law—just to save their pockets! Don't you feel how glorious it would be to prosecute such scoundrels?"

Langley glanced at the glowing face and smiled.

"Yes, I can sympathise with that. But I believe an inspector has to be a man of long practical experience."

"I must make inquiries. I would gladly go and work at some mechanical trade to qualify myself."

"What would Lady Revill think of the suggestion?"

For a moment Louis hesitated. His features were a little clouded.

"I don't think she would seriously object—when she saw my motives."

"But you have told me that such motives make very little appeal to Lady Revill."

"The fact is, Mr. Langley, I am as far from understanding her as she is from understanding me. It would be outrageous ingratitude if I said, or thought, that she has any but the best and kindest intentions. You know, I daresay, how much I owe to her. But there it is; there is no getting over the fact that we can't see things from the same point of view. She isn't by any means an obstinate aristocrat; she can talk liberally about all sorts of things, and I know she has the kindest heart. Well, why should she take such care of *me*, the son of insignificant people, except out of mere goodness? But she has such strong personal antipathies. I've never mentioned it, but she hates the name of Mrs. Tresilian. Now, of course I can't be ruled by such prejudices in her. You don't think I ought to be, do you?''

"It's a delicate point," answered Langley, looking far off. "As you say, you have great obligations——"

He paused, and Louis continued abruptly:

"Yes. That's why I am so anxious not to incur more. That's why I don't want to go to Oxford. I should do her no credit there, for one thing; study isn't my bent. I want to be *doing* something. I seem to be acting inconsiderately, but I feel so sure that Lady Revill will admit before long that I did right. Remember that I don't want to get up in public and rail against all the things she values. I couldn't do that. All I aim at is some work of quiet usefulness; something, too, which will make me independent. When I was a boy it didn't matter so much—I mean my obstinate self-will. Often enough I behaved very badly; I know it, and I'm ashamed of it; but then I *was* only a boy. Now it's very different; and in the future——"

Louis broke off, as if checked by a thought he found it difficult to utter.

"I haven't asked you," he added, when his companion kept walking silently on, "whether you know Lord Henry Strands."

"I knew nothing but his name, until Mr. Worboys spoke of him."

"Did he say——?"

Langley encouraged him with interrogative look.

"I've never spoken about it to Mr. Worboys, and I don't know whether——. But it's so important to me that, if I am to talk of myself at all, I can't help mentioning it. And in Lady Revill's circle I don't see how it can help being talked about. I believe that she will marry Lord Henry."

Langley stopped, but immediately turned his eyes upon the landscape, and spoke as if it alone had arrested him.

"You see the dark mountain top far away there—to the right of

Salamis. That's Akrokorinthos.—Ah, you were saying that Lady
Revill may marry again. And in that case, you think your position
might be still more difficult?''

"If she married Lord Henry Strands. He and I can't get on together.
Now he *is* an obstinate aristocrat, and the kind of man—well, I'd
better not say how I feel towards him. It astonishes me that Lady
Revill can endure such a man. People with titles are often very
pleasant to get on with; but *he*—. I wish you knew him, Mr. Langley. I
should so like to hear what you thought of him.''

"You have no reason"—Langley spoke slowly—"for thinking
that this marriage will take place, except your own surmise?''

"Well—he comes so often. And his sister is so intimate with Lady
Revill. I'm sure it's taken for granted by lots of people.''

"I see.''

Something in the tone of this brevity caused Louis to look at the
speaker with uneasiness.

"I'm afraid you think I oughtn't to have mentioned it.—But really,
it's very much like talking about royal marriages. One somehow
doesn't feel——''

"I meant no reproof,'' said Langley. "Stop; here's a good place to
rest. I see there are a lot of people up at the Chapel.—It's a month
since I was here.''

His eyes wandered over the vast scene, where natural beauty and
historic interest vied for the beholder's enthusiasm. Plain and mountain; city and solitude; harbour and wild shore; craggy islands and the
far expanse of sea: a miracle of lights and hues, changing ever as
cloudlets floated athwart the sun. From Parnes to the Argolic hills,
what flight of gaze and of memory! The companions stood mute, but it
was the younger man who betrayed a lively pleasure.

"What's the use,'' he exclaimed at length, "of reading history in
books! Standing here I learn more in five minutes than through all the
grind of my school-time. Ægina—Salamis—Munychia—nothing
but names and boredom; now I shall delight to remember them as long

as I live! Look at the white breakers on the shore of Salamis.—It's all so real to me now; and yet I never saw anything like these Greek landscapes for suggesting unreality. I felt something of that in Italy, but this is more wonderful. It struck me at the first sight of Greece, as we sailed in early morning along the Peloponnesus. It's the landscape you pick out of the clouds, at home in England. Again and again I have had to remind myself that these are real mountains and coasts.''

Langley roused himself from oppressive abstraction, and put into better words this common sense of mirage due to the air and light of Greece. He spoke deliberately, and as if his thoughts were still half occupied with things remote. The frown imprinted on his features conveyed an impression of gloom; which was rarely its effect.

"How do you like the smoking mill-chimneys at Piræus?'' he asked suddenly.

"Oh, of course that's abomination.''

"Ah, I thought you would perhaps defend it. The Greeklings of to-day would be only too glad if their whole country blackened with such fumes.''

"Well, they have their lives to live. They can't feed on the past.''

Louis apologised with a smile for his matter-of-fact remark; but Langley surprised him by saying abruptly:

"You're quite right. They have their lives to live; and if they *want* mill-chimneys, let them be built from Olympus to Tænarum.''

Wherewith he turned away, and moved a few paces with restless step. Louis followed slowly, his eyes cast down, and did not speak until the other gave him a glance of singular moodiness.

"I'm afraid I often disgust you, Mr. Langley.''

"Nay, my dear fellow; that you have never done,'' was the kindly-toned answer. "I meant what I said. You are right—a thousand times right—in pleading for to-day. It's good to be able to appreciate such a view as this; but it's infinitely better to make the most of one's own little life. I get a black fit now and then when I remember how much of mine has been wasted—that's all.''

Concession such as this from a man he had quickly learned to like and respect stirred all the modesty in Louis.

"My trouble is," he said, "that I haven't knowledge enough to make me feel secure, when I take my own way. I may be blundering as all very young men are apt to do."

"Don't be in a hurry, that's the main thing. Above all, don't act in disregard of Lady Revill."

"That's what I wish never to do," Louis answered fervently. "And I should like to tell you that Mrs. Tresilian has always spoken in the same way. Lady Revill dislikes her—can't bear the mention of her name. She thinks I have got a great deal of harm from Mrs. Tresilian. Not long before I left England, she told me as much, in plain words, and it made me so angry that I said things I'm sorry for now.—I am hasty-tempered; I flare up, and call people names, and that kind of thing. It's a bad fault, I know; but surely it's a fault also to hate people out of mere prejudice."

"You can hardly call it mere prejudice, in this case," objected Langley, walking with head bent again.

"But I do! Lady Revill has never taken the trouble to inquire what sort of woman Mrs. Tresilian is, and what she really aims at. When I told her—too violently, I admit—that Mrs. Tresilian had begged me always to think first of what I owed to my guardian, she simply didn't believe it. Of course she didn't say so, but I saw she *wouldn't* believe it, and that enraged me.—There is no better, nobler woman living than Mrs. Tresilian! Every day of her life she does beautiful, admirable things. Her friendship would honour any man or woman under the sun!"

The listener restrained a smile.

"I can quite believe you. But I am equally convinced that Lady Revill is, in her own way, as good and conscientious. They would never like each other——"

"The fault would be entirely on Lady Revill's side," broke in Louis, now glowing with the ardour of his scarcely disguised passion.

"Mrs. Tresilian is incapable of prejudice; but Lady Revill——"

"You must remember," interposed Langley, "that I once knew her. I don't suppose she has altered very much, in essentials."

"I beg your pardon, Mr. Langley. I am forgetting myself again."

"No, no; speak as you think. It's a long time ago; Lady Revill may have altered very much. You think her hopelessly prejudiced in matters such as this."

"I only mean, after all," said the young man, "that she belongs to her class."

"There's a good deal of enlightenment among the aristocracy nowadays," rejoined Langley, with a smile.

"No doubt. I have seen signs of it here and there. But Lady Revill——"

"Is altogether old-fashioned, you were going to say."

"Not those words; but it's true; she prides herself on being old-fashioned. And really, I should like to know why. It isn't as if she were a silly or ill-educated woman."

Langley laughed.

"After all," he said, with humorous gravity, "the old ways of thinking didn't invariably come of folly or ignorance. Never mind; I know what you mean, and I can sympathise with you. I think it very likely, too, that the habits of her life have prevented her mind from developing, as it once promised to. For many years Lady Revill has taken a great part in—we won't say social life, but in the life of society."

"And the surprising thing," exclaimed Louis, "is that she doesn't care for it."

"Why do you think she doesn't!" his companion asked, with a look of keen interest.

"From observing her at various times. Society far more often bores her than not. I have seen her tired and disgusted after being among people, and she has often spoken to me contemptuously of society life on the whole. That's the contradiction in her character."

"No contradiction, necessarily, of her old-fashioned views."

"I mean," Louis explained, "that despise it as she may, she allows herself to be society's slave. She would perish rather than commit some trifling breach of etiquette. Another inconsistency: she is profoundly religious."

"Life is made up of such incongruities," said Langley.

"Evidently; and they astound me. I believe that if Lady Revill acted on her convictions, she would have to give all she possesses to the poor, and join a sisterhood, or something of the kind. And I really think she is often much troubled by her conscience. All the more astonishing to me that she feels such a hatred of the people who try to carry religion into practice—such as Mrs. Tresilian."

The boy talked on, and Langley kept a long silence.

"On the whole, then," he said at length, absently, "you don't think Lady Revill has found much satisfaction in life."

"Indeed I don't!" Louis replied with emphasis. "And, what's more, I am convinced that if she marries Lord Henry Strands she will have less happiness than ever."

Langley walked on a little, then, as if shaking off reverie, spoke with sudden change of tone.

"I forgot to ask you what Mr. Worboys is doing this morning."

"Oh, he is busy writing-up his notes. It's a tremendous business always."

"Well, I envy him. He has a purpose in life. You and I, Louis, have still our vocations to discover."

It was the first time that he had used this familiar address. The young man reddened a little, and looked pleased.

"You, Mr. Langley!"

"You think me too old to have anything before me?—Do I strike you as a decrepit senior?"

"Of course not," answered the other, laughing. "I meant that I thought your vocation was scholarship."

"Nothing of the kind. I am no more a scholar than you are. To be sure, I like the old Greeks. The mischief is that I haven't paid enough heed to them.''

Louis gave an inquiring glance.

"What do you suppose it amounts to,'' asked Langley, ''all we know of Greek life? What's the use of it to us?''

"That's what I have never been able to learn. It seems to me to have no bearing whatever on our life today. That's why I hate the thought of giving years more to such work———''

"You'll see it in a different light some day,'' said Langley. "The world never had such need of the Greeks as in our time. Vigour, sanity, and joy—that's their gospel.''

"And of what earthly use,'' cried the other, "to all but a fraction of mankind?''

"Why, as the ideal, my dear fellow. And lots of us, who might make it a reality, mourn through life. I am thinking of myself.''

Louis walked on with meditative, unsatisfied smile.

V

**A** DAY or two after this Langley had a morning appointment with Worboys at the Central Museum, where the archæologist wished to invite his friend's "very serious attention" to certain minutiæ of the small copy of the Athena Parthenos. Nearly half an hour after the time mentioned Worboys had not arrived, yet he prided himself on habitual punctuality. Impatient, and beset with thoughts which ill prepared him to discuss the work of Pheidias, Langley loitered among the sepulchral marbles. These relics of the golden age of Hellas had always possessed a fascination for him; he had spent hours among them, dwelling with luxury of emotion on this or that favourite group, on a touching face or exquisite figure; ever feeling as he departed that on these simple tablets was graven the noblest thought of man confronting death. No horror, no gloom, no unavailing lamentation; a tenderness of memory clinging to the homely life of those who live no more; a clasp of hands, the humane symbolism of drooping eyes or face averted; all touched with that supreme yet simplest pathos of mortality resigned to fate. But he could not see it as he was wont, and he knew not whether this inability argued an ignoble turmoil of being, or yet another step in that reasonable unrest of manhood which had come upon him like an awakening after sluggish sleep.

A rapid step approached him. It was Worboys at last, and wearing a look of singular perturbation.

"A thousand apologies, my dear Langley, for this seeming neglect. I couldn't get here before. Something very troublesome has happened. I must beg your advice—your help."

They walked apart, for other visitors had just come within earshot.

"By this morning's post," pursued Worboys, "Louis has had a letter—I don't know from whom, though I suspect—which has upset him terribly. He came to me at once, after reading it, and declared that he must return to England immediately. In vain I begged for an explanation; he would tell me nothing except that go he must, and go he would. Straightway he began making inquiries about steamboats. I am bound to say that he treats me in very inconsiderate fashion. Of course I could not dream of letting him go back alone; my responsibility to Lady Revill is of the gravest. In this state of mind he is as likely as not to fall ill: in fact, when he came to me an hour ago, I thought he was in a high fever. Now, what *am* I to do, Langley? Happily he can't get off to-day, but——"

"Who do you suspect the letter was from?"

"Mrs. Tresilian, that source of all our woes. I'm sure the occasion is unspeakably preposterous. The idea of this lad believing himself in love with a woman of that age and position! And what's the good of his going? Really, one is tempted to imagine very strange things. I shouldn't like to calumniate Mrs. Tresilian——"

"The letter may not be from her at all. Just as likely, I should say, that it is from Lady Revill. Well, I don't see how you are to detain him if he's determined to go."

"Lady Revill will be exceedingly displeased," said Worboys, at the height of nervous exasperation. "In her very last letter she said that we were not, in any case, to return before midsummer, though discretion was accorded me as to how and where we should spend the time. I should be ashamed to face her. It's monstrous that a man in my position should find himself powerless over a boy of eighteen! And to leave Greece just when I am——''

"It's confoundedly annoying," the other interrupted, absently.

"Will you see him? Will you try what you can do?"

"If you don't think he'll bid me mind my own business."

"Nothing of that sort to fear. He always behaves like a gentle-man—in words, at all events. But for that I'm afraid I should never have got on with him at all. He's a thoroughly good fellow, you know; it's only his outrageous excitability, and this unaccountable affair with——. Well, well, as you say, I may be mistaken. But I don't like the way he looks when I plead Lady Revill's directions."

"Does he defy them?"

"Simply declares that he has no power to obey her, but he looks savagely. Will you come to the hotel?"

Langley consulted his watch.

"No. I'll send a note as quickly as possible asking him to come and see me early in the afternoon. Better to let him calm down a little. You say no steamer leaves the Piræus to-day?"

"None. And he's too late for the train that would take him to Patras. He won't sneak off; that isn't his way. It'll all be done openly and vehemently, depend upon it."

They parted, and Langley soon dispatched his note of invitation. At three o'clock, as he sat in the book-cumbered room, smoking his longest pipe—for he wished to receive the visitor with every appear-ance of philosophic repose—Louis joined him. So troublous was the expression of the pale, handsome face; so pathetic its presentment of the eternal tragedy—youth, ignorant alike of itself and of the world, in passionate revolt against it knows not what; that the older man could not begin conversation as he had purposed, with tranquil pleasantry. He rose, offered his hand, pressed the other's warmly, and said, in a grave voice:

"I'm very sorry to hear that you are going away."

"I must. I, too, am sorry, Mr. Langley. But I must go to Patras to-morrow, and leave by the steamer which sails for Brindisi at midnight."

The voice quivered in its effort to express unchangeable purpose without undignified vehemence.

"That's most unfortunate. If we had been longer acquainted I should have felt tempted to ask whether a deputy could save you this trouble, for I myself am leaving for England very soon."

"Thank you, Mr. Langley; it is impossible. I must go."

"Let us sit down. It's no use pretending that I don't see how upset you are. You have had bad news, and your journey will be no pleasant one. At your age, Louis, it's no joke to be travelling for a week with misery for one's companion."

The young man was sitting bent forward, his hands locked together between his knees.

"Nor at any age, I should think," he answered, trying to smile.

"Oh, well, one takes things more resignedly later on. I suppose Mr. Worboys will go with you?"

"He says he feels obliged to. It's too bad, I know. I seem to be acting selfishly. But"—his voice faltered on a boyish note—"I simply can't help it. Something has happened—I can't go on living here—at any cost I must get back to London——"

Gradually, patiently, with infinite tact, always assuming that the journey was a settled thing, Langley brought him to disclose the disastrous necessity. That morning, said Louis, he had heard from Mrs. Tresilian; a short letter, which it drove him frantic to read. Mrs. Tresilian wrote a good-bye. She informed him that a gentleman— name unmentioned—had called upon her with a strange request— that she would hold no more communication with Louis Reed. This person represented to her that, however innocently, she had made serious mischief between Louis and the lady to whom he owed everything, upon whom his future depended. The explanation that followed allowed her no choice; she must say farewell to her dear young friend, though hoping that the severance would not be final. It was her simple duty, out of regard for him, to do so. So she begged that he would not write again, and that, on his return to England, he would not see her.

"And I know who has done this!" the young man exclaimed passionately. "Lady Revill would never have done it herself. I can't believe that she knows of it—I can't! I have told her frankly that I corresponded with Mrs. Tresilian, and she said only that she regretted the acquaintance. No; it's that man I have spoken of to you: Lord Henry Strands."

"That sounds a trifle improbable."

"I dare say, but I *know* it! He has done this, thinking it would please Lady Revill. Of course she tells him everything about me. Well, it only drives me into what must have come before long. I must ask Lady Revill to give me my independence. I shall go out into the world and work for my own living. I'm going back to tell her this."

"And to tell Mrs. Tresilian also, " remarked Langley, with his kindest smile.

Louis averted his face.

"I have told you how I regard her," he said, in a tone of forced firmness. "Her friendship is more valuable to me than—— Why should I be called upon to give it up? The thought of her is the best motive in my life. Without that, I don't know what may become of me. I should very likely go headlong——"

Langley checked the hurrying sentences.

"Don't strike that note, my dear boy. I know what you mean by it, but it isn't in harmony with the rest of you; it isn't manly."

Louis accepted the rebuke; he coloured, and said nothing. Thereupon his friend began to talk in an impressive strain; with gravity, with kindliness that almost had the warmth of affection, with wisdom which would not be denied a hearing. He pointed out that no harm whatever had been done by the officious stranger. Mrs. Tresilian's friendship had merely proved itself anew, and in a way that did her credit. Now, which of two possible courses was the more likely to commend itself to her respect: a wild rush from abroad, with youthful heroics to follow, or a calm, manly acceptance of her own view of the situation, with assurance that their mutual regard could not suffer by a temporary silence?

"If you find anything reasonable in all this, let me go on to make a proposal. For purposes of my own I must go to England, and I may as well start to-morrow as a week hence. I shall see Lady Revill as soon as I arrive. I mean"—he lowered his voice, and spoke with peculiar deliberation—"I have a reason of my own for wishing to see her. It is sixteen years since we met, but our acquaintance was intimate, and there's no possibility of her receiving me as a stranger. Now, will you allow me to speak for you to Lady Revill? No word shall pass my lips which you would disown. Will you stay in Greece, or, at all events, on the Continent, until you have heard from me, and from her?"

He paused, knowing the first reply that trembled on his hearer's lips. Impossible! Louis declared that it would be misery beyond endurance. His relations with Lady Revill had grown intolerable. He could not permit even the kindest friend to act for him in such circumstances.

Langley watched the flush that deepened on the face wrung with impetuous emotions. His sympathy grew painful; he was on the point of saying, "Well, then, we will travel together." But other thoughts prevailed with him; he struggled to support the aspect of equanimity, and talked on with a resolve to impose his reasonable will, if by any effort it might be done. Louis was reminded that the post would still convey his letters whithersoever he pleased.

"I dare say you have already replied to Mrs. Tresilian?"

"Yes."

"And told her that you were coming straightway? Now, if I were Mrs. Tresilian (don't laugh scornfully), nothing would please me better, after receiving that piping-hot epistle, than to get another couched in far more thoughtful language. You don't forget that this admirable lady will suffer a good deal if she is compelled to believe that her friendship has really been a cause of injury to you?"

That stroke told. The young man fixed his eyes on a distant point and became silent. Langley talked on, calmly, irresistibly. Little by little he permitted himself a half authoritative tone, which the listener seemed very far from resenting. Langley had learnt from his sym-

pathetic imagination that the repose of acquiescence would seem
sweet to one in Louis's state of mind, if only perfect confidence were
instilled together with it. He spoke long and familiarly, revealing
much of himself, at the same time that he displayed his complete
understanding of the trouble he strove to soothe. And in the end Louis
yielded.

"In that case," he said, his voice hoarse with nervous exhaustion,
"I can't stay at Athens. I must be moving. I should perish here."

"We'll settle that with Mr. Worboys. You had better go and 'sail
among the Isles Aegean.' Do you know Landor's 'Pericles'? Oh, you
must read it. Here, I'll lend it you. Return it when we meet in
England."

Louis took the volume mechanically.

"I know it will all be useless. You will write and tell me what I
already know. If you imagine that Lady Revill can be persuaded by
reasoning——"

"I don't," interrupted the other, with a peculiar smile.

"I feel convinced, Mr. Langley, that you will find her very different
from the lady you knew so many years ago. Even since I was old
enough to observe such things, I have noticed a change in her; she is
colder, harder——"

Langley still smiled.

"Yet, you say, not happy in her coldness and hardness. Bear in
mind that I am something of an old-fashioned Tory myself; perhaps
we shall find points of sympathy to start from."

"You are the most advanced of Radicals compared with Lady
Revill."

Langley mused.

"By the by," he said, as his companion rose, "there seems to have
been an understanding that you were not to return, in any case, till
after midsummer."

"Yes. And the reason is plain."

"Indeed?"

"It means, of course, that on my return I shall find her married."

"It is the merest conjecture on your part," said Langley, knitting his brows. "As likely as not you are altogether mistaken in that matter."

Louis smiled with youthful confidence.

"We shall see."

His friend moved across the room, and turned again, restlessly.

"You admit that you have absolutely no authority but your own surmises?"

"True, But it's sure as fate—and very wretched fate. I don't speak selfishly; pray don't imagine anything of that kind; I'm not capable of it. Whatever I say of Lady Revill, I"—he hesitated—"I have a son's love for her. And that's why I loathe the thought of her marrying such a man. But for him, with his hateful pride, things would never have come to this pass between us. He has made her dislike me, and I regard him as my worst enemy. She puts me out of her way—she is sorry she ever had anything to do with me—and yet I have no one else——"

The emotion which broke his voice, as far as possible from unmanly complaint, touched the listener profoundly.

"Give me your hand, Louis. I pledge you my word that this shall be settled in some way satisfactory to you. Be of good heart, old fellow, and trust me."

"You will do all that any one can, Mr. Langley."

"Perhaps more than any one else could. We shall see."

VI

I N the morning Langley had a talk with Worboys. The tutor, far from exhibiting jealousy of his friend's superior influence, was delighted at the unhoped-for turn of things.

"It would have cut me to the heart," he declared, "to go away without having visited either Delphi or Olympia. We shall be able to take them on the homeward route. I agree with you that it will be well to spend a week or so in travel among the islands. We will go to Suros (Syra, they call it), whence, I understand, we can get to Delos. Thence to Eubœa, to Thermopylæ, and perhaps as far north as the Pagasæan Gulf (Gulf of Volo, they barbarously name it), which would allow us a glimpse of Pelion."

The greater part of the night Langley spent in packing and letter-writing. His heavy luggage would follow him to England. When he looked around him on trunks and portmanteaux ready for removal, it wanted but an hour of daybreak; from his sitting-room window he saw a pale pearly rift in the sky above Hymettus. Merely to rest his limbs, for sleep he could not, he threw himself on the bed.

"Thanks to you, friend Louis! You have given me the push for which I waited, and it will impel me — who knows how far? Perhaps at this time next year — but that lies in the lap of the gods."

Worboys came to him after breakfast, and announced that Louis would be at the railway station to see him off.

"He looks a ghost this morning, poor fellow. What a calamity to have such nerves! I can't remember that I was anything like that at his time of life. My father used to call me the young philosopher."

They reached the station a quarter of an hour before train-time, and found Louis pacing the platform. Drawing Langley aside, he talked with feverish energy, repeating all his requests and demands of the day before. When the traveller entered the shaky little carriage Louis still kept near to him; silent now, but with anxious eyes watching his countenance. As the train began to move they looked for a moment fixedly at each other. In that moment the two faces were strangely alike.

The line makes a circuit over the plain of Attica, and turns westward through the hollow between Aigaleos and Parnes. Thence, in view of the bay so closely guarded by lofty Salamis as to seem an inland water, it runs to Eleusis, and a railway porter shouts the name once so reverently uttered. A little beyond rise abruptly those jagged peaks which were the limit of Attic soil; and then comes Megara, its white houses clustered over the two round hills; silent, sleepy, ignorant of its immortal fame. On by the enchanted shore, looking now across a broader sea to softly-limned Ægina and the far mountains of Troezene; until the isthmus is reached, and the train passes over that delved link of west and eastern gulfs which the ancient world cared not to complete. *"Non cuivis homini,"* murmured Langley to himself, as he stretched his limbs on the platform at Corinth; gazing now at the mighty bulk of Geraneion, dark, cloud-capped; now at the noble heights of the ancient citadel, Akrokorinthos. Once more he could enjoy these visions, for with movement there had come to him a cheery quietude, a happiness of resolve.

Forward now by the coast of Peloponnesus, through mile after mile of currant fields and olive plantations, riven here and there by deep track of torrents which at times rush from the Achæan mountains.

Through a long afternoon his gaze turned across the blue strip of sea, beholding as in a magic mirror those forms which appear to be bodied forth by the imagination rather than viewed with common sight: Helicon, shapen like a summer cloud, vast yet incorporeal, far-folded, melting from hue to hue; and more remote Parnassus, glimmering on the liquid heaven with its rosy wreath.

At Patras he was in the world again. A clamour of porters and hotel-touts; a drive through choking dust; dinner at a table where he heard all languages save Greek; then the purchase of his ticket for Brindisi. Exhausted in mind and body, he shipped himself as soon as possible, and slept for many hours. On awaking he found himself within sight of Corfu—Corcyra, as he remembered with a smile, thinking of Worboys. But it was the modern world; he could now give little thought to Homer or to Thucydides. In his last glimpse of Parnassus he had bidden farewell to the old dreams. English people were on board, and their talk sounded not unpleasant to him.

Another night (to his impatience, the whole day was spent at Corfu), and he rose early for a view of the Italian shore. There it lay, a long yellow line, whereon, presently, a harbour became visible. Not Brundisium, but Brindisi. A great English steamship was putting forth, bound for India; he watched it with a glow of pleasure, even of pride.

A brief delay at the port, then onward by rail once more. By sunny-golden sands of Calabria, where yet linger the Hellenic names; northward through rugged mountains, to Salerno throned above her azure bay; by the vine-clad slopes of Vesuvius, by the dead city of the menaced shore, into a regal sunset burning upon Naples.

VII

IS arrival in London was at mid-day; the sky heavily clouded, and the streets lashed with a cold rain. Until late in the evening he sat idly at his hotel reading newspapers, but before going to bed he wrote a few lines addressed to Lady Revill. A formal note, constructed in the third person. Would Lady Revill grant an interview to Mr. Edmund Langley, who was newly returned from Athens? No more.

Were the lady in town he might receive an answer by the evening of next day. But the day passed, and no letter arrived for him. A second day went by; and only on the morning of the third was there put into his hand a small envelope, which he knew at a glance to be the reply he awaited. He opened it with nervous haste. Lady Revill apologised for her delay; she was in the west of England, and would not be back in town until Saturday evening. But if Mr. Langley could conveniently call at eleven on Monday morning, it would give her pleasure to see him.

Friday, to-day. By way of killing an hour he wrote to his friends at Athens. It was long since time had dragged with him so drearily, for he did not care to seek any of his acquaintances, and could fix his attention on nothing more serious than the daily news. To his surprise, the last post on Saturday brought him a letter with a Greek stamp. Auguring ill, he struggled with the cacography of Mr. Worboys, which conveyed disagreeable intelligence.

"We were to have sailed from the Piræus for Syra on the afternoon of the day after you left us, but I grieve to say that this was rendered impossible by an attack of illness which befell our young friend. He could neither sleep nor eat, and was obliged to confess—when we had absolutely reached the harbour—that he felt unable to go on board. I felt his pulse, and found him in a high fever. One circumstance contributing to this was doubtless a long and exhausting walk which he took on the day of your departure; if you can believe it, he positively walked for some nine hours, on an empty stomach, returning in a great perspiration long after sunset. This, in one of his constitution, was sheer madness, as I forthwith told him. From the Piræus we returned as quickly as possible to Athens, and medical aid was summoned. Our excellent doctor seems not to regard the crisis as alarming, but he forbids any movement. How often I have tried to impress upon Louis that these southern climates do not permit of the excesses in bodily exertion which may with impunity be indulged in at home! I have telegraphed to Lady Revill, as she desired me always to do in case of illness. I shall send other dispatches from time to time, and you will thus, probably, be aware of what is going on before you receive this letter."

"Poor lad! poor lad!" was the burden of Langley's thought for the rest of the evening.

On the morrow, precisely at the appointed hour, he made his call in Cornwall Gardens. It was long since he had stood at any door with an uncomfortable beating of the heart. The sensation revived, with hardly less than their original intensity, those pains with which he had entered old Mr. Forrest's presence for the fatal interview sixteen years ago.

The door opened, and solemnly, behind a solemn footman, he ascended the stairs, vaguely percipient of the marks of wealth and taste about him, breathing a fragrance which increased the trouble of his blood. In vain he strove to command himself. It was like the ascent of a scaffold; every step lengthened his physical and mental distress.

A murmur of the footman's voice; a vision of tempered sunlight on many rich and beautiful things; a graceful figure rising before him. It was over. The mist cleared from his eyes, and he was a man again.

Lady Revill received him with grave formality, almost as though they met for the first time. He had not expected her to smile, but her absolute self-control, the perfection of her stately reserve, excited his wonder. On him, it was clear, lay the necessity of breaking silence; but the phrases he had prepared were all forgotten. Their greeting was mere exchange of bows; he must plunge straightway into the business which brought him here.

"I have just returned from Greece." A motion bade him be seated, and he took the nearest chair. "At Athens I encountered by chance an old friend of mine, Mr. Worboys, and thus I was led into acquaintance with Mr. Louis Reed."

Lady Revill sat still and mute. When the speaker paused, she regarded him with an air of expectancy which puzzled Langley; it was an intense look, calm yet suggesting concealed emotion.

"I am sorry to hear," he continued, straying from a tenor of speech which threatened to be both stiff and vague, "that Mr. Reed fell ill just after I left. I had a letter on Saturday from Mr. Worboys."

The lady spoke.

"I received a telegram on Friday. Mr. Reed was then better; but his illness, I fear, has been dangerous."

Her voice reassured Langley, so nearly was it the voice of days gone by. In face and figure Lady Revill retained more of youth than he had allowed himself to expect; on the other hand, her beauty appeared to him of less sympathetic type than that which his memory preserved. She was thirty-seven, and, like most handsome women who have lived to that age amid the numberless privileges of wealth, had lost no attribute of her sex; feminine at every point, she still, merely as a woman, discomposed the man who approached her. Yet her features had undergone a change, and of the kind that time alone would not account for. Langley defined it to himself as loss of sweetness, for which was substituted a cold dignity, capable of passing into austere pride. This was independent of her gravity assumed for the occasion; he saw it inseparable from her countenance. He felt sure that she did not often smile. In silence her lips were somewhat too closely set—a pity, seeing how admirable was their natural contour.

She was so well dressed that Langley had no consciousness of what she wore, save that it shimmered pearly-grey. Her hair had not changed at all; now as then, she well understood how to make manifest its abundance, whilst subduing it to the fine shape of her head. Her hand bore only two rings, the plain circlet and the keeper; its beauty was but the more declared.

"I knew nothing of this illness when I wrote asking your permission to call. But it was of Louis that I wished to speak."

Again he saw the singular expectancy in Lady Revill's look. Her eyes fell before his scrutiny. He continued.

"When I learnt that he was your ward, I of course felt a greater interest in him. I told him I had known you before your marriage, and in that way we quickly formed a friendship. It is as his friend that I must now venture to speak to you. I came to England with this purpose, after persuading him, with great difficulty, to give up an intention he had of coming hurriedly back himself. The news of his illness hardly surprised me. I left him in a terribly excited state—the result of a letter he had received from London."

Langley talked on without constraint, but not without an uncomfortable sense that he must appear impertinent in the eyes of the mute, grave listener. Her coldness, however, had begun to touch his pride; he felt the possibility of braving considerations which would have embarrassed him seriously enough even had Lady Revill betrayed some tenderness for their common memories.

"A letter from me?" she asked, in deliberate tones.

"From Mrs. Tresilian."

A shadow crossed her face. Her lips grew harder.

"In a boy's spirit of confidence," Langley pursued, "he had talked to me of Mrs. Tresilian, whom I know only by name. He had told me that he regarded her as a very dear friend, and told me also that it was a friendship of which his guardian disapproved. Then, one morning, Mr. Worboys asked me to aid him in opposing this resolve. I did so, and successfully, but not until Louis had told me the facts of the case. Mrs. Tresilian had written to him that their friendship must come to an end, the reason being that she had learnt how distasteful it was to you. A gentleman, unnamed, had called upon her, and begged her to make this sacrifice out of regard for the young man's welfare."

With satisfaction he perceived that his narrative was overcoming the listener's cold reserve. It became obvious that Lady Revill had no knowledge of these details.

"I cannot think," she said, "that any one known to me has behaved in that strange manner."

"Louis had no choice but to believe his friend's explanation. I thought it probable that he had written to you on the subject."

"He wrote a very short and vehement letter. But it contained no word of this." She paused for an instant, then added, "All he had to say to me was that he begged me to grant him his independence, that he wished to go forth into the world without assistance or advice from any one, and more to the same effect. I have had such letters from him before."

"You can understand now how he came to write in that strain."

Langley spoke, in spite of himself, with less scrupulous respect than hitherto—somewhat curtly. On Louis's behalf, he resented Lady Revill's unsympathetic tone.

"I can understand," she said, "that the person whom he calls his friend may have wrought cruelly upon his feelings; but I repeat that no acquaintance of mine can possibly have had any part in the matter."

Langley reflected, and controlled his tongue, which threatened to outrun discretion.

"In any case, Lady Revill, his feelings *were* cruelly wrought upon, and to that the poor boy's illness is due. May I speak now of something that had entered my mind even before this event? Louis talked a good deal to me of his position and of his aims. You will do me the justice to take for granted that I in no way encouraged him in discontent. On the contrary, I did my best to keep him reminded of how young he was, and how inexperienced. Happily there was no need to insist upon the deference he owed to your wishes; on that point he showed a right feeling. But at the age of eighteen, and with a temperament such as his, it is difficult always to act unselfishly, or even rationally. Whatever the source of it, he is possessed with a resolve to be—as he puts it—of some use in the world. You know the meaning of that formula on the lips of a young man nowadays. He is going through the stage of hot radicalism. Education for its own sake seems to him mere waste of time. The burden of the world is on his shoulders.''

Langley's smile elicited no response. But Lady Revill had abandoned her statuesque pose, and her countenance reflected anxious thoughts.

''Mr. Worboys,'' she remarked coldly, ''seems to have been unable to influence him.''

''Quite unable, though I should say that travel had not been without its good effect. Mr. Worboys has too little understanding of his pupil's mind.''

''What were you about to suggest, Mr. Langley?''

''Nothing very definite. But I think I can enter into Louis's feelings, and I seemed to attract his confidence, and this suggested to me that I might be of some service if other influences failed. I know that I am inviting a rebuke for officiousness. A word, and I efface myself again. But if you permit me to serve you, I would gladly do all I can.''

''The difficulty is very great,'' said Lady Revill, ''and I feel it as a kindness that you should wish to help me. But how? I am slow to catch your meaning.''

''All I should ask of you would be a permission to continue, with your good will, the relations with Louis which began at Athens. I am an idle man, without engagements, without responsibilities. When

Louis comes home, would you consent to my taking up, informally, the position Mr. Worboys will relinquish? It would give me a purpose in life—which I feel the want of—and it might, I think, afford you some relief from anxiety.''

Lady Revill sat with eyes cast down; she kept so long a silence that Langley allowed himself to utter his impatient thought.

"You don't like to say that you think me unfit for such a charge?''

"I had nothing of that sort in mind, Mr. Langley,'' she answered, in a lowered and softened tone.

"You shrink from restoring me, thus far, to your friendly confidence.''

"That is not the cause of my hesitation.''

Langley winced at this reply, which was spoken with a return to the more distant manner.

"In brief, then,'' he said quietly, "my offer is unwelcome, and I must ask your pardon for venturing it.''

"You misunderstand me. I am very willing that you should act as you propose.''

It seemed to him, now, that Lady Revill assumed the tone of granting a suit for favour. Moment by moment her proximity, her voice, regained the old power over him, and with the revival of tender emotion he grew more sensitive to the meanings of her reserve.

"But,'' he remarked, "you foresee a number of practical difficulties?''

Very strangely, she again kept a long silence. Her visitor rose.

"I ought not to ask you to decide this matter at once, Lady Revill. Enough if you will give it your consideration.''

"It is decided,'' she made answer, rising also, but with a hesitation, all but a timidity, which did not escape Langley's eye. "My difficulty is that I must acquaint you with certain facts concerning Louis which I don't feel able to speak of in this moment.''

"If you will let me see you at another time——''

"Do you remain at the hotel?''

"For the present. I have no home."

"Believe, Mr. Langley, that I feel the kindness which has brought you here."

She seemed of a sudden anxious to atone for cold formalities. Her face, he thought, had a somewhat brighter colour, and the touch of diffidence in her bearing was more perceptible.

"If you knew how glad I am to speak with you once more——"

Suppressed emotion at length betrayed itself in his voice, and he stopped.

"I will let you hear very soon," said Lady Revill.

She offered her hand, and Langley at once withdrew. When he had left the house it surprised him to find how short the interview had been, and he was puzzled at the abruptness of its termination. He had imagined that they would talk either for a mere five minutes or for a couple of hours.

VIII

UT the worst of his suspense was over. He could now seek such congenial acquaintances as he had in town, and look to their society with the relish born of long solitude. Never a man of many friends, he knew himself welcome at all times in certain households of good standing; and for some years he had belonged to one of the most agreeable of literary clubs. It was early in the London season; a man who felt that he had somehow entered upon a new lease of life could not do better, whilst grave possibilities hung in the balance, than live as London prescribes to those who have means and leisure, taste and social connexions.

First of all, however, he dispatched a letter to Louis Reed; a letter warm with the kindest sympathy, and full of hopeful suggestiveness. All was going well, he assured Louis, and news more definite should come before long.

He thought it likely that some days would elapse before he heard from Lady Revill; and so, when he rose on the following morning, he had no special anxiety to inquire for letters. But on entering the coffee-room, he saw that the unexpected had happened; there was a letter for him, and from Lady Revill. Having given his order for breakfast, he broke the envelope. It contained several pages of writing, which, to his surprise, did not begin with any form of epistolary address; at the end, he saw, stood merely the signature, "Agnes Revill." In one whom he believed so careful of conventionalities, this seemed strange. Hastily he glanced over the first page; then he folded the letter, and cast a glance about him a glance of bewilderment, of apprehension, as though afraid of a stranger's proximity. Catching a waiter's eye, he rose, and directed that his breakfast should be kept back till he again ordered it; then he went upstairs to his bedroom.

Sunshine flooded the room. Standing with his back to the window, and so that the morning glory streamed upon the paper in his hand, he read what follows:—

"In the autumn of 1877, a year after my marriage, I went to spend a fortnight with my parents, at their home. Whilst staying there, I heard, in family talk, that a middle-aged couple who were old friends of ours, their name Reed—people in a humble position, whom I think you never met, and perhaps never heard spoken of —had recently adopted a child, a little waif of three years old. I called upon them, and they told me, as far as they knew it, this child's history.

"A few years before, a young and parentless girl, whom they had known since her childhood, had disappeared from the town; her name was Eliza Morton. Suspicion arose that she had gone away with a man named Hollingdon, a commercial traveller, and some attempts were made to discover her where-abouts, but these efforts failed. But in the summer of 1877, Mrs. Reed one day received a message from the young woman, who had returned to the town, and lay ill at a lodging-house. Mrs. Reed went to see her, and found her in a dying state. The woman said that she was married, and to the man who had been suspected of leading her astray; the child she had with her, a little boy, was the offspring of this union. Hollingdon had taken her abroad, to South Africa, where eventually he deserted her, but not without leaving her sufficient means to return to England. For twelve months she had been in failing health, and it was with difficulty that she reached her native town. Fearing she might not recover, she appealed to Mrs. Reed on behalf of the child, whose name, she said, was

Percival Louis Hollingdon. After a consultation with her husband, Mrs. Reed consented to take charge of the child should the mother die—an event which happened a few days later.

"The Reeds thought it doubtful whether the young woman had really been married; she wore a wedding-ring, but evaded questions as to the date and place of the ceremony. That, however, did not affect their promise on the child's behalf. Childless themselves, they were very willing to adopt this poor little boy, whose intelligence and prettiness made him interesting for his own sake. So he was taken into their home. As Mrs. Reed had no liking for the name Percival, she decided to use the child's second name, and call him Louis. For patronymic he received their own, and so grew up as Louis Reed.

"As years went on, I frequently saw this child, who grew much endeared to his adoptive parents. When he was seven, Mrs. Reed died. Her husband survived her for two years only, and in broken health. Shortly before his death, in 1882, I went to see him, and on this occasion he revealed to me a fact which had been known to him for about six months—a fact relating to Louis Reed's origin. He said that he had received a visit from the man Hollingdon, who, newly back from wanderings over the world, was making inquiries in the town concerning his wife, and had been directed to Mrs. Reed. On learning all that had happened, Hollingdon declared that the dead woman had spoken falsely in saying that her child was his also. It was true that he had married Eliza Morton, but only after she had lived, in London, with another man, to whom she had borne a child. He affirmed that, out of love for the girl, who had broken with her 'protector,' he permitted her to take the child when they were married and went abroad together. Subsequently, he confessed, he deserted his wife, partly because he wished for a child of his own, and felt jealous of her devotion to the little boy. Asked if he knew the name of this boy's father, he said that it was Langley.

"There seemed no reason to doubt the story. The dying woman had doubtless been ashamed to confess the whole truth to her friends; she wished to leave an honourable memory, and thought, no doubt, that she was doing the best thing for her child. With its father she either could not, or would not, communicate.

"As you have interested yourself in Louis Reed, I felt it necessary to inform you of these circumstances. On Mrs. Reed's death, I made myself responsible for the boy's future. A small sum of money was left for his use when he should come of age. Mrs. Reed had had him well taught at a day-school, and his education proceeded much as it would have done had he been my own child. During the last three years, he has regarded my house as his home, and me as legally his guardian. He knows that the Reeds were not his parents, having learnt that from the talk of his early schoolfellows; and on the one occasion when he asked me about his origin, I thought it the wisest course to profess total ignorance. From Mr. and Mrs. Reed, it appears, he had learnt nothing on this point."

After this came the simple signature.

An hour elapsed before Langley left the room, and went down to breakfast. The unobservant waiter remarked no change in him, but in truth the interval had changed his aspect wonderfully—had lent his features the vivacity of youth, and given him a lighter step, a more animated bearing. As he sat at the breakfast table and affected to read the newspaper, his vision was more than once dimmed with moisture; he smiled frequently.

After the meal, he wrote to Lady Revill, and, in imitation of her example, omitted epistolary forms.

"Will you let me see you very soon? May I come to-morrow morning, at the same hour as yesterday?—Edmund Langley."

He was engaged to lunch at Hampstead, and he walked all the way thither from Trafalgar Square; it seemed the pleasantest mode of passing so fine a morning. For he had an unfamiliar surplus of energy to work off, and the buoyancy of his spirits could not find adequate play save in the open air and the sunshine. After his climb up the northern heights, finding that he would have half an hour to spare, he

executed a purpose which had only come into his mind when the
beginning of fatigue enabled him to think more soberly; he went to the
post-office and wrote a telegram addressed to Worboys at Athens.
"Send me news of Louis without delay." This dispatched, he walked
on in meditation. "All danger was over some days ago," ran his
thoughts. "But I must know how he is. And to-morrow evening—
yes, to-morrow evening—I start for Greece again!"

His hostess, a charming woman, as she talked with him after
luncheon, paid a merry compliment to the health and brilliancy he had
brought back from the classic land. Langley, absorbed at the moment
in his own thoughts, said, as though replying:

"Do you know Mrs. Tresilian?"

"A singular question! Has she any credit for your air of happiness?"

"I am not acquainted with her, but I wish to find some one who is."

"Be your wish fulfilled. I know Mrs. Tresilian, and have known her
for years."

"Yes," said Langley, with a smile, "I am fortune's favourite. Pray
tell me something about her."

"Oh, she is delightful. Dine with us on Sunday, and I think I can
promise you shall meet her."

"I shall probably be thousands of miles away. But what can you tell
me of Mr. Tresilian?"

"Monsieur is a most estimable man," answered the lady, with a
face of good-humour. "Somewhat older than his wife, it is true, but a
model of the domestic virtues, and sincerely respected by all who
know him—though I am bound to say they are few. His passion is for
agriculture; he lives for the most part on his farm in Norfolk."

"And Mrs. Tresilian prefers the town?"

"She is a citizeness of the world, and lives wherever she can do
good. I am quite serious. A great deal of nonsense is talked and
believed about her. She is 'advanced,' but I wish all women were
equally to the fore in work and spirit such as hers."

"I am very glad indeed to hear this," said Langley, in a grave tone. "I thought it probable."

"Oh, generous man! How your view of probabilities becomes you!"

"I am getting old, remember. Let the young enjoy the privilege of cynicism. And yet there are young people, even in our day, who can think with the generosity which ought to be the note of youth."

"Happily," returned the hostess, "I know one or two—girls, of course."

"Of course? Not a bit of it. I was thinking of a noble-spirited boy."

He dropped his eyes, for they dazzled.

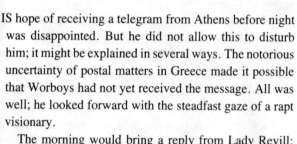

IX

IS hope of receiving a telegram from Athens before night was disappointed. But he did not allow this to disturb him; it might be explained in several ways. The notorious uncertainty of postal matters in Greece made it possible that Worboys had not yet received the message. All was well; he looked forward with the steadfast gaze of a rapt visionary.

The morning would bring a reply from Lady Revill; and in this his confidence was justified. She expected him at eleven o'clock.

When he entered the drawing-room, it was vacant. He moved about, glancing at the pictures and other objects of interest; and presently his eye fell upon a photograph of Louis, which stood on a table. An excellent likeness; he regarded it with such intense delight that he was not aware of the entrance and approach of Lady Revill; her voice, bidding him good morning, called his startled attention, and he took with unthinking ardour the hand she offered.

"Have you any news from Athens?"

"None." She withdrew her hand, and retired a little, but did not sit down. "As the last telegram was so reassuring, I feel no uneasiness."

Her demeanour had more suavity than on the former occasion. Still reserved, still clad in her conscious dignity, and speaking with the voice of one who has much to pardon, she manifested relief; and

Langley felt no check upon the impulses which demanded utterance.

"I telegraphed yesterday morning, but there was no reply when I left the hotel. No news is of course good news. As soon as I have heard, I shall start."

"For Athens?"

"Yes."

They exchanged a look. Lady Revill did not invite him to be seated, and her wandering eyes, as she stood in the unconsciously fine attitude of a tall, graceful woman, expectant, embarrassed, explained the neglect of forms.

"Why have you kept this from me?" he proceeded. "But for an accident, should I never have known it?"

"Perhaps, never. Perhaps, when Louis attained manhood."

"May I hope to know your reasons?"

"You do not doubt the truth of the story on which it all depends?" she asked, without regarding him.

"How can I doubt it? Every detail in your narrative is true—so far as they come within my own knowledge."

"Yet no suspicion crossed your mind—at Athens?"

"How could I have been led to such a thought? The name— Louis—but then it wasn't the name by which his mother called him—the name of her own choosing. And the fact of your guardianship; was *that* likely to turn my suspicions towards the truth?"

Lady Revill cast a glance towards Louis's portrait on the table.

"Did no one with whom you were in company perceive a personal likeness?"

"Worboys seems not to have observed anything of the kind. Is there a likeness?"

He turned to the photograph, and then again to Lady Revill, with a light of ingenuous pleasure on his face.

"I don't understand," she answered coldly, "how the resemblance escaped any one who saw you together."

Langley smiled, with difficulty repressing a laugh of joy.

"Mr. Worboys lives in the ancient world; modern trivialities make no impression upon him. And this likeness confirmed you in the belief of what you had been told?"

His voice, vibrant with glad feeling, fell to a note that was almost of intimacy.

"I am surprised," said Lady Revill, taking a few steps and laying her hand upon a chair, "that the revelation seems so welcome to you."

"It is more to me than I dare tell you," he answered with a fervour which seemed to resent her lack of sympathy. "How you yourself feel towards Louis, I cannot know; yet you must have some understanding of what it means to a man very much alone in the world when he finds that Louis is his own son."

"Have you ever tried to discover what had become of the child?"

"Never. Will you forgive a question I am obliged to ask you in return? It is this: Did your parents speak of me to you, when I went away, with absolute condemnation? or did they offer any excuses for my behaviour in their house? I took care that my story should be made known to you. But will you let me know in what shape it was related?"

Lady Revill seated herself; Langley remained standing. The great joy that had befallen him overcame his oppressive self-consciousness; and the thought that this beautiful woman, whom in his heart he still named "Agnes," had for years been mother to his son, gave him a right of intimate approach not to be denied by her stateliest gravity.

"I only knew," was her distant answer, "that you had a responsibility which forbade your marriage."

"That is extremely vague." He began to speak as one who demands, rather than requests, an explanation. "Besides, it was not true."

"How can you say that?" Lady Revill looked upon him for an instant with surprise. "You have acknowledged the truth of what I put in writing."

"There was no responsibility that forbade marriage. When I told your father my story, he took time to think about it, and I then heard from him that it was deemed impossible to speak to you of such things. I accepted this decision, but only for a day. Then I understood that respect for your parents must not make me unjust to myself—and perhaps to you. When I wrote, at length, asking you to be my wife, I wrote at the same time to your father, telling him of the step I had taken, and requesting that you should be informed of all I had let him know. It seemed my only course: rightly or wrongly, our habits forbid a man to speak of such things to the girl he wishes to marry. Is it possible that your father, in replying that you had heard 'everything,' did not tell the truth? I know what crimes good people will commit in the name of morality; but surely Mr. Forrest was incapable of such transaction with his honour?"

The listener's countenance grew fixed as a face in marble. Langley, unheeding its frigid reproof, went on.

"Did you know *all* the facts? Or only that I was father of a child? Or perhaps not even as much as that?"

The statue spoke.

"I knew of the child's existence. It was enough."

"From my point of view, far from enough. You were never told that the child's mother, of her own desire, had married another man and taken the child away?"

"The knowledge could not have affected my opinion."

It was spoken with undisguisable effort. Langley, watching her face intently, saw a quiver of the brows and of the hard-set lips.

"Ah, then you did *not* know. In telling you so much, and no more, your parents did me a grave wrong."

"Mr. Langley, your own wrong-doing was so much graver that I cannot see what right you have to reproach them."

His blood was now warm; his pride rose in contest with hers.

"In a case like this, Lady Revill, the question of right or wrong can only be decided on a most intimate acquaintance with the circumstances."

"I think otherwise. Admission of one fact is enough."

"There we are at issue, and I daresay neither of us would care to argue on the subject. But in one respect your natural kindness has overcome the severity of your creed. You did not visit upon the child the sins of the father."

Lady Revill was silent.

"If you had condemned me," proceeded Langley, "because I neglected my duty to the boy, I could have said little enough to excuse myself. There, indeed, I was guilty. The circumstances made it difficult for me to act otherwise than I did; but none the less I threw aside carelessly the gravest responsibility that can be laid upon a man. In your view, no doubt, it was my first duty to marry the mother. To have done that would have been to lay the foundation of life-long misery. My selfishness—if you like—saved me from worse than folly. But it is true that I ought not to have given up the child to an unknown fate. The mere ceremony of marriage is of no account; but a parent is bound by every kind of law in the interests of his child."

A movement in his hearer checked him. Turning, he saw that a servant had entered the room. The man silently approached, and presented a salver on which lay a telegram.

"I think this is from Athens," said Lady Revill, when they were alone again.

Langley waited, his pulse quickened with expectation. He watched the delicate hands as they broke the envelope, saw them unfold the paper, saw them suddenly fall.

"What news——?"

Her eyes had turned to him. In their stricken look in the blanching of her cheeks and of her parted lips, he read what lay before her.

"Will you let me see?" he said quietly.

She gave him the telegram.

"Grieve to say that Louis died this morning. Painless and like a sleep. Please let me know your wishes."

He looked to the sunny window, but saw nothing. Dark wings seemed to beat over him, and chill him with their shadow. Lady Revill had risen; the sound of a sob escaped her, and she trembled, but her eyes were tearless. Then Langley faced her again.

"I must reply at once. What is your wish, Lady Revill?"

"My wish is yours. Would you like him to be brought to England?"

"Why? What does it matter?" he answered in a hard voice.

"It is yours to decide."

Her utterance echoed the note of his. They stood regarding each other distantly, their faces stricken with a grief which they strove to master.

"Let him be buried among the ruins," said Langley, with bitter emphasis.

He laid the telegram on a table; stood for a moment in hesitancy; turned to his companion.

"Good-bye."

Her lips moved, as if to speak the same word; but another sob caught her breath. Commanding herself, she flashed a look at him, and said impulsively:

"Do you lay it to my charge?"

Langley was over-wrought; a flood of violent emotion broke through all restraint.

"Why have you stood for years between me and my son? What right had you to withhold him from me?"

"I see no shadow of right in your reproach. You cast him off when he was a little child. What claim had you upon him when he grew up?"

"Again you speak in ignorance of what happened. It was against my will that I let his mother take him away. She could pretend no love for me, but she loved her child, and I was unable to refuse her. There was an understanding that, if ever she needed help, she would let me know. In acting as she did, afterwards, she broke her promise to me. I foresaw the possibility of what came about. She knew how to communicate with me. The child would have been brought up under my care. But she wished to die in the odour of respectability."

"And does your conscience acquit you in all other respects?" Lady

Revill asked, she, too, the mere mouthpiece of tumultuous feelings. "Have you no thought of the first sin — the source of all that followed, including your misery now?"

"Say what you will of that," he answered scornfully. "The moral folk of the world take good care that what they choose to call crimes shall not go unpunished, and then they point to an avenging Providence. You, no doubt, in keeping my son from me, considered yourself to be discharging a religious duty. You feared, perhaps, that his father would corrupt him. If the boy had died before I saw him, you would have written me a letter, pointing the moral of the tragedy. You have robbed me of years of happiness. And how much happier would *his* young life have been! As it was, you condemned him to a struggle with conditions utterly unsuited to his nature. Your prejudices of every kind, your lack of sympathy with all that is precious to a generous young mind in our time — did no perception of this ever trouble you? Perhaps, after all, I was wrong in what I granted just now. Perhaps you knew all that the boy was suffering, and accepted it as the penalty he had to pay for his father's vileness?"

"You don't know what you are saying!" exclaimed the other, shrinking before his vehemence, and now gazing at him with sorrowful rebuke.

"What reason had you?" He stepped nearer. His face had aged by many years, and showed wrinkles hitherto invisible; his eyelids were red and swollen, as though from weeping. "How do you justify yourself, Lady Revill?"

"The child was not yours," she answered, with troubled breath. "You gave him up to his mother, and it was her right, when dying, to choose what guardian she would."

"Even so, *you* were not the guardian chosen. When you learnt the truth from Mrs. Reed, it was your duty to communicate with me. — But you are right; I am talking wildly and foolishly. Nothing can be undone. The boy lies dead at Athens. Let him be buried there — among the ruins."

As he once more turned from her, his eye fell upon Louis's portrait.

He moved toward it, and stood gazing at the ardent face; then, without looking round, said in a thick voice:

"Have you one of these that you can give me?"

"Take that. There are others that you shall have."

"Is there one taken long ago—when he was a little boy?"

"Several. You shall have them."

"Tell me this—speak frankly, plainly. Had you any true affection for him?"

"Why else should I have treated him as though he were a child of my own?"

"Did you? That is what I want to know. Or was it only the conscientious discharge of what you somehow came to think your duty?"

Lady Revill looked at him with searching eyes.

"Did he speak," she asked, "as if I had behaved to him without affection?"

"He spoke of you with respect."

"With nothing more?"

It was all but a cry of pain, and Langley subdued his voice in answering.

"Remember that we were strangers to each other; mere acquaintances, it seemed, and of such different ages. Remember, too, that he was at the time of life when a boy's simplicity is out-grown, and the man's thoughtfulness has not yet developed. I found in him—and it is saying much—not a trace of ungenerous feeling. He spoke with regret of the trouble and anxiety he had caused you."

"Never heartlessly," interrupted the listener. "Never in a way that could make me sorry I had——"

Her voice broke; she bent her head.

"He said more; and judge of the strength of his feeling, that he could overcome a boy's shame, and speak of such things. He confessed to me, in his bitterness, that he loved you with a son's love; and lamented that you had lost all kindness for him."

"It was not true! How could he think that?"

"What is the use of love that is never shown?"

"He turned from me—he made friends of people who taught him to rebel against my wish in everything."

"You were mistaken," said Langley. "I know who you are thinking of. That friend of his, from first to last, spoke no word disrespectful to you. She did not even know that you had found fault with him on her account. And when some one or other told her how serious the matter was getting, you know how she wrote to him."

"An easy magnanimity."

"It is you who seem to find the reverse of magnanimity so easy. I know nothing of this woman, except what I heard from Louis. Public report is worthless; though you, doubtless, make it the whole ground of your prejudice against her. I believe that she did act magnanimously, or at all events in honest kindness; out of regard both for him and for you. I know a lad can be fooled by the most worthless woman, but this is no such case."

"I bring no charge against her," said Lady Revill, coldly, "except that the result of her influence, whether she proposed it or not, was to set Louis's mind in opposition to all I desired."

"What did you desire?"

She seemed to disdain an answer.

"Perhaps," Langley went on, without harshness, "you had some memory of me—of views I used to hold—and your intention was to make of him a man as unlike me as possible. I am not what I was—unhappily. Life has killed off so many of my enthusiasms, as it does in most men. You did me the honour, perhaps, of imagining me still warm on the side of poor wretches—still cold to the aristocratic ideal. You sought to repress in the boy all that did him most credit— his unselfish aspirations, his bright zeal for justice and mercy—his contempt for idle and conceited worldlings. I once knew a woman who would never have done that—but the world has changed her."

"You talk in utter ignorance of me," Lady Revill replied.

"Whatever your motive, the result was the same."

Emotion again shook her.

"I tried to do my duty, and you are the last person who should reproach me if I mistook—if I failed to make his boyhood a time of happiness——"

"His life, said Langley, after a few moments of painful silence, "was not unhappy. His troubles came of no idle or shameful cause, and he was full of purpose. If he could have grown up at my side! If I could have led him on, taught him, watched the growth of his mind— what a companion! what a friend! And I have wasted my life, idled and sauntered through the years, whilst, unknown to me, that duty and that happiness lay within reach!"

Lady Revill gazed at him appealingly through tears.

"No," he continued, with a gesture of impatience, "I shall not forget myself again. I spoke in maddening pain; it was true, I didn't know what I said. I am ashamed to have spoken to you like that—to you. You had reasons for what you did; never mind what they were."

Again there was silence, and Lady Revill sank wearily upon a seat.

"Shall you go to Athens?" she asked.

"What use—to see a grave? But yes; I shall go."

"You do wish him to be buried there?"

"Yes. In the little cemetery by the Ilissus. Ah, you know nothing of all that."

"Is it beautiful—like the cemetery at Rome?"

"No; not in that way. A poor little patch of ground. But it lies close by the ruins of a great temple, and at evening the shadow of the Acropolis falls upon it. He was learning to love Athens; and if I could have gone back to him—. I should have started to-night. In a week I thought to be with him again."

When he paused Lady Revill asked under her breath:

"You would at once have told him?"

"You think I should have shrunk from it," he answered, with a revival of scornful emotion. "Oh, how the proprieties imprison you!"

How the pretty hypocrisies of life constrain the nobler part of you!''

"To you, then," she exclaimed, a hot flush upon her cheeks, "all decency, all shame, is the restraint of hypocrites?"

"No; but the false feelings that take their name. You would think it more becoming, I dare say, to have let him remain fatherless, than to confess that, twenty years ago, I was young, and had a young man's passions."

"Poor boy! I can hardly grieve that he is dead."

"At least, that is logical," said Langley, with answering bitterness, "for you would have liked him to feel a misery worse than death in the knowledge of his birth. And perhaps he would really have felt it. Perhaps the influence of his education, the moral lessons you have assiduously taught him—. Oh, let us make the best of what can't be helped; let us be content that he is dead."

Lady Revill rose from her chair.

"Mr. Langley, shall I reply to this telegram, or will you do so?"

"I will do so, in your name."

"Thank you."

It was a dismissal. Langley glanced at the photograph, but did not take it. Lady Revill, however, moved quickly, and put it into his hand.

"Your grief is very bitter," she said, in a shaken voice.

Their hands just touched, and he left her.

X

HE day passed in a moody and fretful indecision. There was a telegram from Worboys, repeating the words of that addressed to Lady Revill; he carried it about with him, and read it times innumerable. The photograph he had put away; but the face it represented came before his mind persistently, and, by a morbid trick of the imagination, changed always to a deathly rigidness, with eyes closed and sunken cheeks.

From harassed sleep, he awoke when it was yet dark, and the sudden return of consciousness was a shock that left him quivering with shapeless fears. He did not know himself, could not recover his personality. It was as though a man should turn to the glass, and behold the visage of a stranger. So much had crowded into the two brief yesterdays: a joy undreamt, the glowing forecast of a life's happiness, a stroke of fate, and thereupon that whirling hour that made him think and speak so wildly. Trying to remember all he had said, he was racked with something worse than shame. It seemed impossible that a moment's anguish could so disfigure a ripened mind, stultify the self knowledge of philosophic years. What foolish insults had he uttered? It was like the behaviour of crude youth, stung into recklessness by a law of life unknown to him.

When day broke, he rose, half dressed himself, and sat down in the twilight with pen and paper.

"For all my frenzy of yesterday, I beg your forgiveness. I owed you gratitude, and behaved with brutality. Will you write a few words, and say that you can make allowance for what was spoken at such a time? Do not think that revealed myself as I am; that was the spirit of long years ago, which in truth I have outlived. Forgive me, and tell me that you do."

Whilst it was still very early, he went out and posted this. An hour after, there came regret for having done so; and through the morning he wandered miserably about unfamiliar streets.

Early in the afternoon, he despatched a telegram to Hampstead, asking for the address of Mrs. Tresilian. No sooner was it sent than he remembered that a glance at a Directory might perhaps have saved the trouble; so forthwith he searched the volume. "Tresilian, Frederick James," no other of the name appeared; and this gentleman's house was in Connaught Square. But Langley could not be sure that it was the residence of the lady he sought; after all, he must await the reply from his friend. It arrived in an hour's time, and astonished him.

"Mrs. Tresilian's address—34, East Lane, Bermondsey."

Was she, then, even more enthusiastic in her cause than he had imagined? Did she positively dwell among the poor?

After brief hesitation he took a hansom, and was driven towards the glooming levels of South-east London. In Bermondsey the cabman had to ask his way. When East Lane was at length discovered Langley alighted at the end, dismissed his vehicle, and explored the by-way on foot. He found that No. 34 was a larger house than its neighbours; it had recently undergone repairs, and looked not only clean, but, to judge from the windows, comfortably furnished. In answer to his knock appeared a very pretty woman, very plainly dressed, whose face, unless he were mistaken, declared her name.

"I wish to see Mrs. Tresilian."

"Will you come in?" was the pleasantly toned invitation; and he followed to a sitting-room on the ground floor, a room simple as could be, but at the same time totally unlike the representative parlour of Bermondsey. There the pretty woman faced him with, "I am Mrs. Tresilian."

"My name is Langley——"

He could add no particulars, for at once his hostess exclaimed vivaciously:

"And you have come from Greece! You have been with Louis Reed!"

"Yes."

"But how did you find me? Louis doesn't know of this place, does he?"

Langley explained, and Mrs. Tresilian laughed at what she called the perfidy of their Hampstead friend.

"I know all about you from a letter of Louis's. How is he? Not ill, I hope?"

The pause which Langley made, and his dark look, alarmed her. In a few words he told what had befallen. The listener, clasping her hands in a gesture of sincere grief, stood for a moment voiceless; then her eyes filled.

"Oh, poor boy! poor boy! Do you know, Mr. Langley, what great friends we were? Oh, and I expected so much of him. He seemed so——"

She had to turn away. Langley, choking with a gentler sorrow than he had yet felt, regarded her through tears that would not be restrained. Often he had smiled at the name of Mrs. Tresilian, knowing only of certain extravagances which served to caricature her personality in the eye of the world; he saw her now as she had appeared to Louis, admiring scarcely less than he sympathised.

"Tell me about him, Mr. Langley. Was he quite well when you left him?"

"In fair health, I thought. But——" He changed the form of his sentence. "Did he not write to you very recently?"

She exhibited much distress.

"Yes. I had a letter only a day or two ago. And how unhappy it will always make me to think that—— Do tell me all you know. You seem to keep something back. If he said anything to you—I will explain my reasons——"

Langley related the events of his last two days at Athens, and the listener sat with bent head, her tears falling. When he ceased she made an effort to calm herself; then, with perfect simplicity, made known the reason for what she had done. It was a sacrifice imposed by her genuine affection for Louis. She had never known, until some one authorised to speak came and told her, that Louis's guardian looked with the strongest disapproval upon their friendship; the matter was represented to her so very gravely that there seemed no alternative, though it broke her heart to write as she did. And Louis's letter in reply was so manly, so noble——

"He wrote so?" Langley interrupted eagerly.

"How proud I should be to show you the letter, if it were not too sacred! And I seem to have only just read it, fresh from his hands. How is it *possible* that the poor boy can be dead? I can't believe it!"

"You speak, Mrs. Tresilian, of some one who came to you with authority. Now, when I mentioned this fact to Lady Revill, she utterly denied that any friend of hers could have taken such a step."

"Then I must justify myself, at any cost," answered the other, with dignity. "The gentleman who called was Lord Henry Strands. He came to the house in Connaught Square—it was the day before I left to come here—and went so far as to tell me in confidence that Lady Revill would shortly become his wife. Of that, Mr. Langley, I am sure you will not speak. I must tell you, for I can't bear that you should think I acted frivolously."

Langley kept silence. His habitual frown expressed a gloomy severity, and Mrs. Tresilian seemed unable to move her eyes from him.

"Are you well acquainted with Lady Revill?" she asked, diffidently.

"Till the other day it is years since we met."

"What I have said surprises you?"

"No. I have heard of Lord Henry Strands. But," he added slowly, "it is clear that he came to you without authority from Lady Revill."

"There seems no doubt of that." Mrs. Tresilian's eyes, still moist, gleamed with indignation. "I know Lady Revill only by name, but I have heard people say all sorts of pleasant things of her. Of course I was sorry to know how she thought of me, but I could not for a moment, considering Louis's age, countenance him in disregarding her wishes."

"Can you—forgive me for questioning you further—can you tell me anything of Lord Henry Strands?"

"I know nothing of him. He looks a man of forty, and seems well-bred, though perhaps a little conscious of his rank."

Their eyes met for a moment, and Mrs. Tresilian again seemed to discover something in the visitor's face which strongly held her attention.

"Do tell me, if you can," she continued, "whether it's true that Lady Revill has a *very* bad opinion of me?"

"She has conservative prejudices."

"And do you suppose that Louis had lost any of her favour on this account? Believe me, Mr. Langley, I never had a suspicion of it. He never spoke to me of any such thing."

"I fear there is no doubt that they differed on this point."

"And perhaps for that very reason he was sent abroad? Oh, how cruel it is! I must think myself in part the cause of his death!"

Her tears flowed again. But Langley, in his kindest voice, endeavoured to reassure her, representing that the actual and sufficient cause of Louis's being sent to travel was the young man's disinclination to enter upon a University career. For this self-will, as he knew, Mrs. Tresilian could in no way be held responsible; Louis's radicalism had begun to flourish before ever he met with her.

"You felt a great interest in him, I am sure?" said the lady, presently; and again her look fixedly encountered his.

"It was inevitable," Langley answered, in a low voice, "after once talking with him."

Their conversation lasted for an hour; before they parted Mrs. Tresilian explained the meaning of her residence in East Lane. She belonged to an informal sisterhood, who had recently undertaken to live, two or three together, and in turns, among this poor population, for example and for help. They kept no servants; all the work of the house was done by their own hands. Each of them took up her abode here for three weeks at a time.

"But I never spoke of it to Louis," she said sadly. "I ceased to tell him of such things when I found that it disturbed his thoughts. He was so good and generous. He wished to be doing something himself. But it was his time for study, and——Oh, but I shall always reproach myself! I did harm, great harm!"

Langley, standing in readiness to take his leave, murmured a few words of deep feeling; and as they shook hands Mrs. Tresilian looked into his face with eyes that thanked him.

XI

HEN the next morning brought no letter from Lady Revill, Langley ground his teeth; he keenly repented his haste in sending off that passionate plea for her forgiveness. What was to be expected of a woman dyed to the core in conventionality?—the widow of Sir Thomas Revill—the plighted wife of Lord Henry Strands! In asking pardon he had been untrue to himself. Heaven forbid that he should have outlived that spirit of revolt which so offended her little soul! If to-morrow he heard nothing he would write once more, and in a more self-respectful strain; then back to Athens, to stand by his son's grave.

But in the evening came a reply. It was written on black-edged note-paper of the finest quality, and couched in terms of irreproachable correctness. "Dear Mr. Langley," it began. Yes; she would no longer countenance informalities; he was henceforth to be an acquaintance like any other. "This afternoon I am leaving town again, to stay for a time at my house in Somerset. You would no doubt like to have some of the things that belonged to Louis, such as books and papers; these shall be put at your disposal when you return to England. Moreover, as you know, I am trustee of a small fund which would have been his when he came of age; in this matter your wishes will be consulted by my solicitors. Believe me, dear Mr. Langley, faithfully yours,——."

How gracious! What delicate regard for his feelings!

He sat late in the smoking-room, turning over newspapers. His hand fell upon a journal of society, and he wondered idly whether it contained any mention of the names in which he was interested. Here was one. Lord Henry Strands, said a rumour, had it in mind to purchase the house in Hyde Park Gardens, vacant since the death of So-and-so. To be sure; a natural step. And, a little further on, the polite chronicler announced that Lady Revill had returned to town for the season, having spent the greater part of the winter at her delightful country home in the west of England. The name of her estate was Fallowfield, and it lay near the interesting and beautiful village of Norton St. Philip, in Somerset, celebrated as having been the resting-place of the ill-fated Duke of Monmouth just before the battle of Sedgmoor. With other particulars; but on the leading point the news-man for once was wrong.

Norton St. Philip. To that part of England, Langley was a stranger. With purposeless curiosity he reached for Bradshaw, but the name of the village did not appear in the index. An out-of-the-way place. The estate had probably belonged to Sir Thomas. Langley yawned, and went to bed.

In the morning he paid an early visit to his club, and for the sole purpose of consulting a gazetteer or guide-book. He found that the village of Norton St. Philip lay some three miles from a little place named Wellow, which was a station on the Somerset and Dorset railway, only six miles from Bath. Again he referred to Bradshaw. The 1:15 express would land him at Bath by 3:30; and thence, after waiting an hour and a half, he could reach Wellow by half past five. He sat musing, and frowning, till the clock pointed to eleven; then returned to his hotel. Here again he mused and frowned, till nearly noon.

At one o'clock he drove up to Paddington, with a travelling-bag. The first part of his journey passed without pleasure or impatience; he watched the telegraph-wires in their seeming sway, up and down, up and down; saw the white steam of the engine float over green meadows; and was at Bath before he had time to unfold his newspaper. An unobservant stroll in the town, and a meal for which he had no appetite—though fasting since formal breakfast—killed the moments until he could proceed. At Wellow he found himself amid breezy uplands. There was no difficulty in procuring a conveyance to Norton St. Philip. He liked the drive, and liked, too, the appearance of the old inn, a fifteenth-century house, which at length received him.

Not till night had fallen did he go forth and ramble in the direction of Fallowfield, some half-hour's walk along a leafy road. Having looked at the closed gates, and the lighted windows of the lodge, he rambled back again. At bedtime he thought of nothing in particular—unless it were the Duke of Monmouth.

But the shining of a new day quickened his life. When he opened his window, spring breathed upon him with the fragrance of all her flowers, and birds sang to him their morning rapture. He no longer marvelled at the impulse which had brought him hither, but smiled to think that he had so much more of resolute manhood than in the prime of youth.

When the sun was high, he again walked over to Fallowfield, and by inquiry at the lodge ascertained that Lady Revill had in truth returned from town. By a winding drive of no great length he approached the house: a most respectable structure, which declared the hand of a Georgian architect. The garden at all events was beautiful, and lovely in their new leafage were the trees that stood about.

In the imposing hall, he waited with no less painful tremor than on presenting himself at the house in Cornwall Gardens. When led at length into a room, he saw with satisfaction that it was no chamber of state, but small and cosy, with windows that opened upon a little lawn. Here again he had to endure some minutes of solitude, marked by heart-throbs. Then sounded a soft rustle behind the screen which concealed the door, and Lady Revill advanced to him. She wore a garb of mourning, admirable of course in its graceful effectiveness, and somehow, despite the suggestion of grief, not out of harmony with the bright spring day. Unsmiling, yet with the friendly welcome which became her as a country hostess, she offered her hand.

"I am so sorry that you should have had to make such a journey to see me. I thought you had left England. If I had known that there was anything you wished to speak of immediately——"

The civil address struck Langley mute. He had not imagined that, face to face with him, Lady Revill would adhere to the conventionalities of her last letter.

"Could it not have been done by correspondence?" she added, as they seated themselves.

"I had no choice but to come. I couldn't go away without seeing you again. The memory of our meeting in London is too painful to me."

Her mood, it seemed, was gentle, for she listened with bent head, and answered softly.

"Hadn't we better forget that, Mr. Langley?"

"I cannot forget that I gave you cause to think very ill of me."

"No. I have no such thought." She was gravely kind. "I did not reply directly to your letter, because I felt sure that you would understand my omission to do so. The blow that fell upon you was so sudden and so dreadful."

"But upon you also it fell," said Langley, when she paused.

"More heavily than perhaps you are willing to believe."

He searched her face for evidence of this, and a moment elapsed. Then, with a collected manner, Lady Revill again spoke.

"As the opportunity offers, let me ask whether you have seen Mrs. Tresilian."

"I called upon her."

"Before leaving town, I had a letter from her. We don't know each other, and I have never wished to know Mrs. Tresilian; but she wrote, seemingly, in great distress, reproaching herself with having contributed to Louis's fatal illness. Whether there can be any truth in that, I am unable to decide. As it was from you, I find, that she learnt the particulars, I am afraid you left her under the impression that she was to blame.''

''I tried not to do so.''

''In this letter,'' proceeded Lady Revill, ''Mrs. Tresilian repeats what I was so surprised to learn from you, the story of some one having called upon her in my name. Please tell me, Mr. Langley, whether this was mentioned in your conversation.''

''We spoke of it,'' he answered steadily.

''I believe I have a right to ask what you learnt from Mrs. Tresilian.''

Langley faced the challenge, admiring the stern beauty of his questioner as she uttered it.

''Certain facts were mentioned in confidence,'' he said. ''But it can hardly be a breach of confidence to repeat them—to you. The gentleman who called upon Mrs. Tresilian was Lord Henry Strands.''

''Thank you.''

Their eyes met unwaveringly. On Lady Revill's cheek mantled a soft glow, but she continued in the same voice, melodious always, though in the note of royal command.

''Did Lord Henry Strands offer any explanation of the step he had taken?''

''He did.''

''Kindly tell me what it was.''

''In confidence, he told Mrs. Tresilian that you would shortly be married to him.''

''Thank you.''

The colour had died out of her face. Without venturing even a glance, Langley waited for her next words; he could not surmise what they would be, for her ''Thank you'' was uttered in an uncertain, absent tone, very unlike that of the interrogator.

''It was not true,'' she said at length, coldly.

He raised his eyes. In the same moment Lady Revill stood up, and spoke once more with the self-possession of a friendly hostess.

"Would you like to see the gardens? If you will wait a moment."

Quickly she reappeared with covered head. She talked of flowers and trees, but her voice sounded to him only as distant music; he answered mechanically, or not at all. A direct question recalled him to himself.

"Do you return this afternoon?"

"I am uncertain. I haven't thought about it."

Utterly confused he could only stare at the shadow upon the grass. Lady Revill walked on, and again drew his attention to some detail of gardening. Able at length to answer in ordinary tones, he met her look, and for the first time she smiled. A smile of no meaning; the mere play of facial muscles trained to express suavity.

"You are alone here?" he asked.

"At present. But I am expecting guests this afternoon—two little nieces, who will stay for a few weeks with me."

Reviving his recollections of her family, Langley was about to ask whose children these were; but Lady Revill spoke again, and on another subject.

"Will you tell me something of Mrs. Tresilian? I am afraid I have done her injustice. Probably I have been misled by public opinion. You are well acquainted with her?"

"Not at all. I had never met her before."

He continued vaguely; careful to avoid specific eulogy, yet suggesting a favourable estimate. And even whilst speaking, he was dissatisfied with himself, for he knew that to any one else he would have given a much bolder description of Mrs. Tresilian. Conscience rebuked him for cowardice.

Conversing thus, they had passed through a shrubbery, and reached an open spot, sheltered with larch trees, where stood a small building of no very graceful design. Lady Revill explained that it was a mortuary chapel, built by the original owner of Fallowfield to contain his wife's tomb. The family was Roman Catholic. Nothing of general interest marked the interior; it had been converted to the uses of

Protestantism, and a clerical guest or the incumbent of the parish, occasionally read service here.

"This path," she added, with her hand upon a little wicket which opened into the consecrated spot, "leads through the plantation to the high road—in the direction of the village."

Was it a dismissal? Langley stood in miserable embarrassment; he seemed to have lost all his tact, all his breeding; he could behave neither as a man of the world nor as an impassioned lover. A boobyish boy could not have been more at a loss how to act or speak. Then he saw that Lady Revill was again smiling.

"Will you give me the pleasure of your company at luncheon?" she said.

This excessive courtesy restored command of his tongue. He answered, in a matter-of-fact phrase, that he feared the time at his disposal was too short; he had better follow this path to the village.

"I mentioned in my letter," began Lady Revill; and then paused, her eyes wandering.

"Thank you; it was very kind. You will let me write to you—when I have decided where I shall live."

She offered her hand, gravely; the dismissal was now in form. Without word of leave-taking, Langley touched her fingers, and passed through the little gate.

XII

E travelled back to London. With no intention of remaining there, and with no settled purpose of going further;
rest he could not, and the railway journey at all events
consumed what else must have been hours of intolerable
idleness. For the fire that so long had slept within him,
hidden beneath the accumulating habits of purposeless,
self-indulgent life, denied by his smiling philosophy,
thought of as a mere flash amid the ardours of youth—
the fire of a life's passion, no longer to be disguised or
resisted, burst into consuming flame. He had accus-
tomed himself to believe that his senses were subdued by
reason, if not by time; and nature mocked at his security.
No hapless lad, tortured by his twentieth year, suffered keener pains
than Langley through the night that followed.

It was solace to him that Lady Revill had expressly declared herself
a free woman. The very fact of her having done so seemed to crush his
hope: for the dismissal that fell from her lips signified, more probably
than not, a passing anger with the indiscreet Lord Henry; she would
shame the man and bring him to his knees, but only for the pleasure of
forgiving him. Such a suitor was not likely to have so far presumed
without solid assurance; and Agnes Revill was not the woman to cast
away, for so trifling a cause, the hope of high dignities.

A few days passed, and in the meanwhile he again communicated

by telegraph with Worboys. The archæologist made known his intention of remaining in Greece; he had written to Lady Revill, and at the
same time to Langley. Thereupon Langley addressed Lady Revill in a
formal letter, asking her wishes with regard to the marking of Louis's
grave. The reply leaving him free to act in this matter as he chose, he
wrote to Worboys that the grave should remain, for the present,
without stone or memorial.

In less than a week—it seemed to him that he had struggled through
a month—the goad again drove him westward. He reached the old inn
at Norton St. Philip, and under cover of darkness prowled about the
precincts of Fallowfield. The next morning, as he strayed with falter-
ing purpose along the high road, an open carriage passed; in it sat Lady
Revill with two little girls. Whether she saw him or not he was unable
to determine. Perhaps not, for she was leaning back, and had an
inattentive air. But this glimpse of her face fevered him. He returned
to the inn and wrote a letter, which, after all, he shrank from dispatch-
ing.

Shortly before sunset he walked along the path by which, a week
ago, he had left Fallowfield. It was too late for an ordinary call at the
house; he half purposed delivering his letter to a servant, that Lady
Revill might read it and think of it to-night. He passed through the
larch plantation, where birds were loud amid the gold-green branches,
and on coming within sight of the little chapel lingered wearily. If he
meant to approach the house from this point he must wait till gloom
had fallen; there was too much risk of encountering some one in the
gardens.

He leaned against a trunk.

The sun went down; the birds grew silent. Possessed by unendur-
able longing he moved forward. But daylight still lingered, and
courage to enter the gardens failed him. Pausing by the chapel door, he
laid a hand upon the ring, and turned it; the door opened, not without
noise, and as he was about to enter a figure rose in the dusk. His heart

lept. Lady Revill had been either sitting or kneeling alone, and now she faced the intruder.

He drew back, closed the door, and stepped aside. In two or three minutes he heard the door creak as it again opened. Lady Revill came forth, and stood looking in his direction. Then, with a few quick steps, he advanced towards her.

"Mr. Langley, why are you here?"

"Because I can't live away from you. Because it is so much harder, now, to relinquish the best hope of life than it was years ago."

Question and answer were uttered rapidly, on hurried breath. Gazing steadfastly on the face before him, Langley saw that it was pale and discomposed; the eyes seemed to bear marks of tears.

"Then," she rejoined in the same moment, "I must tell you at once, without choosing phrases, that you are guilty of strange folly."

"That may well be. But the folly has too strong a hold on me. I am sorry to have broken in upon your privacy; but very glad to have met you. Of course I had no idea you were in the chapel."

"You ought not to be here. It's unworthy of you; and if I am to live in fear of being surprised whenever I come out alone—. What more have we to say to each other?"

"If only you will hear me! When one has wasted so many years of life, ever so faint a hope of recovering the past becomes a strong motive."

"Wasted? Why have the years been wasted?"

She endeavoured to speak with her usual cold dignity, but her voice had lost its firmness. Langley could not take his eyes from her; pallid, disdainful, with tormented brows, the face had a wonderful beauty in this light of afterglow.

"Why?" he echoed sadly. "Folly, of course. But the natural enough result of what we both remember."

"And whose the blame?" broke from her lips. "Whose the blame?"

"Who is ever to blame for spoilt lives! Fate, I suppose: a convenient word for all the mistakes we live to be ashamed of."

"Convenient for those who can think so lightly of a crime. Your *mistake*! And what of the other lives that it condemned to unhappiness?"

"Yours, at all events," said Langley, with downcast eyes, "did not suffer from it."

She looked scornfully at him, and answered with bitter irony.

"That thought must be a comfort to you."

"Why not?" His face was suddenly agleam. "What life can have been happier than Lady Revill's?"

"Only your own, perhaps. Oh, is it worth while to waste our sarcasm on each other: You can say nothing that I care to hear. If the best of life is over, so is the worst, thank God! Let us remember that we are man and woman, and respect ourselves."

"It is because I have learnt to respect myself—the strongest, truest desire of my life—that I am here."

"At my cost!" she uttered passionately. "Do I find pleasure in remembering all the misery you brought upon me?"

"Surely you are a little unjust. If your life has been unhappy, are not you in part to blame for it yourself? You don't talk of fate; you account us responsible for what we do."

"With your views, it isn't to be expected you should understand me. What can you know of the revolt against my own feelings—the disgust with life. Oh, how can *you* know what passes in the mind of a girl who loses at once all faith and hope?"

"My views," answered Langley, with gentleness, "allow me to imagine all that. They allow me, also, to compare your acts and mine. It would be easy to flatter you by taking all the blame upon myself. Men generally do so; it helps, they think, to make life possible. They do it 'out of respect for women.' But I can see in it nothing respectful; much the reverse. It is as good as saying that a woman cannot be expected to see facts and to reason upon them. On my side there was wrong-doing; let that be granted. But what of your marriage? Excuse it as you may, was it not worse than what *I* had to avow? You plead outraged feelings, loss of faith and hope, driving you, I suppose, into a sort of cynical worldliness. I, on the other hand, plead my youth and manhood—a far more valid excuse."

She stood motionless, avoiding his eyes.

"And it is idle to pretend," he went on, still quietly, "that you can judge me now as you did then. It is worse than idle to stand before me as an injured woman, austere in her rectitude. Whatever *I* have to regret, *you,* Lady Revill, have yet more."

The dusk thickened. A breeze stirred in the larches. Lady Revill cast a sudden look in the direction of the house, and moved a few steps; then paused, and faced her companion again.

"You came to tell me this?"

"No. To tell you that the love you rejected is stronger now than then. I could not do so whilst I thought that you loved another man."

"You never thought it."

"I could not suppose that Lord Henry Strands spoke falsely."

"Nor did he. I had given him every reason, short of absolute promise, to believe that I would marry him. But what has marriage to do with love?"

"Little enough, I dare say, as a rule. Perhaps I have no right, even now, to speak to you as if you were a free woman?"

"Oh, I am free." She laughed. "Free as ever I was."

"If so, I have more to say. After all, I *can* honestly take upon myself the blame for all that happened. If only I had not been such a pedant in morals! I was absurd, when I thought myself nobly honest. I had no right whatever to make known what I did."

Lady Revill met his eyes, and for a moment reflected.

"You not only had the right," she answered, "but it was your plain duty."

"But think. Your parents did not deal honestly with me—nor with you. You were not told the whole truth. And I might have foreseen that. They wished to guard you from me."

"It would have made no difference."

"Perhaps not—and yet I think it would. You were not a girl of the brainless kind. You condemned me because I seemed to have acted with vulgar unscrupulousness; whereas I had fulfilled every obligation."

"You never offered to marry her."

"Thank heaven, no!" He went on vehemently. "Are you determined to echo the silliest cant? What sort of marriage would that have been? Have we not known of such? You are speaking in defiance of all that life has taught you. I, when I committed that folly of telling your father an irrelevant fact, at all events believed myself to be compelled in honour to do so. But you, with your knowledge of the world, degrade yourself when you repeat mere moral phrases, wholly without application. Neither for the mother's sake, nor for the child's, ought I to have married her: and you know it. It was my plain duty to marry the woman I loved—who let me hope that she loved me in return. I ought to have said not a word of things past and done with."

"But they were not done with."

"Yes; in any sense that could have affected our marriage. Suppose, when you had been my wife for a long time, you had learnt of the poor boy's existence—even as you did. Can you wrong yourself so utterly as to pretend that this would have troubled our happiness? I know you too well. You are not a woman of that kind."

Again she turned, and moved a few paces. Her hands hung clasped before her.

"One thing you have said truly," were her next words, in a low, sad voice. "My parents did not deal honestly with me. They owed me the whole truth. Still, it would have made no difference."

"At the moment, perhaps not. But it would have saved you from that marriage; and in a year or two——"

"You can't understand. We see life so differently."

Langley stepped towards her.

"That is what I don't believe. You hoodwink yourself with the old prejudices, which you have long outgrown, if only you could bring yourself to confess it. Listen, Agnes.'' She shrank, startled; but he repeated the name, just above his breath. ''By your own admission life has satisfied you just as little as it has me. We both see it from much the same point of view; we both look back on a dreary failure. You have lived in slavery to all manner of conventional hopes and fears— playing your part well, of course—but a part of which you were weary from the day you undertook it. You have had social success, honour—and hate the memory of it. I—well, you know the course that I have followed. Not even my flatterer could name it a 'career.' A life of sluggish respectability. Oh, infinitely respectable, I assure you! An immaculate life, by the ordinary standard; and what a waste of golden, irrecoverable time! If you and I had met in the year after your marriage, and in a flood of passion had braved everything—going away together—defying the sleepy world: how much more worthy of ourselves than this honourable ignominy!''

''You forget yourself.''

''I have forgotten myself too long. It was Louis who awakened me, taught me how low I had sunk. Did his bright young life never excite the same feeling in you? Was conscience really on your side when you tried to shape him to the respectable pattern?''

She raised her hands, as if in appeal, and let them fall again.

''Since I met you again, I have learnt how much of youth there is still in me. Shall I give up my dearest hope, as I did so many years ago? You too are young; and you have learnt the worthlessness of mere social ambition. Isn't it true? Another upward step was before you; a higher title; but the cost of it was a lie—and you *could* not!''

''Yes; that is true,'' she answered, softly.

''And the poor boy—hadn't he a part in it?''

She kept silence. Dusk was passing into clouded night; the breeze in the larches sang more loudly.

''You have not told me why you kept him to yourself, and treated him as a child of your own.''

''One often acts without reasoned motive.''

"But in looking back—in recalling the time when you must have debated with yourself——"

"I did wrong," she uttered impulsively. "Forgive me for that—forgive me, and let us say good-bye."

"No! I said good-bye once, to my sorrow. Agnes, in a new life——"

He tried to take her hand, but she withheld it, and spoke with sudden firmness.

"I shall not marry again. I have made it impossible, and purposely."

"How? You fear the judgment of your world?"

"I fear nothing, but the voice of my own conscience—I can't talk about it; my mind is made up. I shall never marry again. I have said all I *can* say; now we must part."

"And you will waste your life to the end?" he said, distantly.

Lady Revill flashed a glance at him, and spoke with nervous tremor.

"Waste? Why need my life be wasted? Is there no hope for me apart from your society?"

"If I answer what I think"—an involuntary laugh broke the words—"none! If I didn't believe that you and I were destined for each other, I should not be here. I believed it long years ago. I believed it again, when I talked of you at Athens. And I have believed it more strongly than ever since the grief we have suffered in common. Nothing that you have said destroys my confidence."

"Then words have no meaning."

"You have made marriage impossible—how?"

"Marriage with *you* was long ago made impossible, by your own act."

"Evasion; and you don't believe what you say. Not my act, but the false light in which it was shown to you. I dare to say that you loved me, and I was not as unworthy of you as you were made to think. Let your tongue be as frank as your heart, and say that you wish for the old time back again, with clearer knowledge. And you have it!"

"I must leave you."

"To go and sorrow that the world, or your own false pride, forbids you doing as you would. Presumption, you call it? I dare everything, for your sake as well as my own. I know how strong it is—all I have to overcome. If I had been bolder, then, how different our lives! I ought not to have accepted your refusal. I ought to have spoken with you, face to face, and told you all with my own lips. Then, even if you had still refused me, you would never have married the man you did not love. I have more courage now. You know what might be said of me—a man with just a bachelor's income. Do I care? I know that *you* can have no such thought. You do not doubt for a moment the sincerity of my love. And but for habit—pride——"

"Yes, if it will convince you. Nothing you can ever say will prevail against them."

"Agnes, you are too proud to live on in the old way. You will respect yourself. The foolish hum-drum of such a life as you have led——"

"My life is my own. I have better use for it than to surrender it into another's hands. It is true that I shall live no longer in the old way. I shall have few friends. Mr. Langley, will you be one of them?"

Her voice was soft, but implied no submission. It sounded weary, and Langley, after a moment's silence, offered his hand.

"Will you let me see you again?"

"If you give me your word that it shall be only as a friend. And not soon. Not till you have been to Athens again."

"I can't promise that. Let me see you in a month's time."

Lady Revill turned towards the house, but looked back, and spoke hurriedly.

"You give me your word not to try to see me for a month?"

He promised, and the next moment stood there alone. Through the deep shadow of the trees, he made his way to the meadow path. Before him, in the western sky, glimmered a rift of pale rose, severing storm-cloud. The burning heat of his temples was allayed; then a sudden chill ran over him, and his teeth chattered.

XIII

E had caught a cold, and spent a sufficiently miserable fortnight in getting rid of it. His spirits were not improved by the arrival of a long letter from Athens, giving him a full account of Louis's illness and death. On the day after receiving it, he sent this letter to Mrs. Tresilian; for it contained mention of her. "If I don't get over this," Louis said, at the moment of the unexpected relapse which rapidly proved fatal, "tell Mrs. Tresilian that to the end I thought of her just as I wrote last."

On recovery, Langley was for two or three days the guest of his friends at Hampstead, and there occurred his next meeting with Mrs. Tresilian. They walked together in the pleasant garden, and conversed with an intimacy like that of long acquaintance. From talk concerning Louis, the lady passed to a kindred subject.

"A week ago I heard from Lady Revill—a very kind and very surprising letter. Perhaps you already know of it?"

"An answer to a letter you wrote——?"

"No. I did write, almost immediately after you came to see me; I couldn't help doing so. The answer to that came quickly—a few lines of very formal politeness, telling me nothing at all. I was the more surprised when I heard again. I could hardly believe what I read. Lady Revill wished to know whether it was in her power to help in the work with which my name was connected."

"A week ago?"

"Ten days, perhaps. What does it mean? A friend had told her something about the Bermondsey settlement, and it interested her greatly. Personally she could do nothing; but if a stranger might be allowed to offer help in the shape of money——. Of course it was worded very nicely, and in the upshot it amounted to this, that our society might draw upon her to any extent! I was really at a loss. Can you explain?"

Langley shook his head, smiling.

"But you, I have no doubt, are the 'friend' she mentioned."

"Lady Revill asked me for some account of what you were doing. I didn't foresee anything of this kind. It was hardly the sort of offer you could accept, I suppose?"

"I thought a great deal about it. We, down yonder, are in no particular want of money; it's personal assistance we need. I wrote at some length, explaining this. I added, however, that there were enterprises in which I took an interest, which wanted as much money as could be got. In a day or two I heard again; just as nice a letter. It's a wretched thing that people misunderstand each other so, just because they are never brought in contact. I thought Lady Revill detested me, and my opinion of her—well, it was not favourable. From poor Louis's talk, I got the idea that she was in many ways an excellent woman, but narrow-minded, and rather arrogant. Her first note confirmed it. But now she writes in the most amiable spirit; with something the very reverse of pride. What does it mean?"

"I can only suppose that Louis's death has touched the better part of her nature."

After a pause, Mrs. Tresilian asked:

"How is Lord Henry Strands likely to regard this change?"

"Impossible to say."

Langley spoke in a tone of indifference, and the subject was dropped.

"Could you dine with me on Thursday, next week?" said the other,
presently. "In Connaught Square, I mean, not in East Lane. My
brother will be there. I am sure he would like to know you; he's a good
scholar, I believe, and has travelled in the East. Nowadays he lives
at——" She named a town of the North Midlands. "He goes in for
municipal affairs, and sometimes signs his letters to me—'Paul the
Parochial.' He takes a pride in his provincialism, and really I think
he's doing a lot of good work. Do you know the town at all?"

"Never was there."

"Paul seems to have unearthed all the local talents," went on Mrs.
Tresilian, in her mirthful spirit. "He rails against centralisation,
persuades the large people to live at home and be active—and so on.
A good deal of Ruskin in it, of course, but he has ideas of his own.
Will you come on Thursday?"

"I will, with pleasure."

It was an odd experience when, among the little group of people
assembled for dinner at his friend's house, Langley found at least three
whose names had long been held by him in contempt or abomination.
There was a political woman, from whose presence, a short time ago,
he would have incontinently fled; this evening he saw her in a human
light, discovered ability in her talk, and was amused by her genial
comments on things of the day. A man known for his fierce oratory in
connection with "strikes," turned out a thoroughly good fellow,
vigorous without venom, and more than tinctured with sober reading.
The third personage, an eccentric offshoot of a noble house, showed
quite another man at close quarters than as seen through the medium of
report. After the society in which, when he saw society at all, his time
had chiefly been spent, Langley tasted an invigorating atmosphere.
These people, one and all, had a declared object in life, and seemed to
pursue it with single-mindedness. But most was he pleased with Mrs.
Tresilian's brother; in many respects, as five minutes' talk assured
him, a man after his own heart: refined, scholarly, genial. This
gentleman began by speaking of Louis Reed, whom he had met only

once, but whose qualities he discussed with such sympathetic insight, such generous appreciation and kindly regret, that the listener had much ado to command his feelings.

He found an opportunity of private speech with his hostess, and inquired whether Lady Revill was still in the country. Mrs. Tresilian thought so.

"I should like to meet her," she added, "but I still feel doubtful of my reception if I appeared before her in the flesh. We have again exchanged letters—to the heaping of more coals upon my head. Her deference really shames me. The rascal that is in all of us—in all women, that is to say—laments that I am not a professional organiser of sham charities. What an opportunity lost! You know that I don't talk of this to every one," she added gravely, "I feel sure that her motive is one which you and I are bound to respect."

Not many days had now to elapse before Langley would be released from the promise which forbade him to approach Fallowfield. He lived impatiently, but the gloom was passing from his mind, and hope grew one with resolve. An effort enabled him to interpret the "month" liberally; he waited till the close of the fifth week, then wrote to Lady Revill, and begged permission to see her. His reason for writing before he journeyed into Somerset was a suspicion that Lady Revill would not be found in her country home; it surprised him not at all when her reply came—with only the inevitable delay—from the house in Cornwall Gardens. In friendly phrase, he was invited to call next day.

On entering, he saw with surprise that the hall was stripped of its ornaments, and all but bare. No hour having been mentioned, he had come in the afternoon; but plainly he need not fear the presence of ordinary callers. From somewhere within echoed the sound of hammering. A maid-servant admitted him; proof that the regular establishment had been broken up.

From the drawing-room had vanished all pictures and *bric-à-brac*; only the substantial furniture remained. Langley tried to recognise a good omen, but chill discomfort fell upon him, and Lady Revill's countenance—she stood waiting in the middle of the room—did not support his hope. She smiled, indeed, shook hands with show of cordiality, and began at once to apologise for the disorder about her; but this endeavour to seem cheerfully at ease put no mask upon the pain-worn features.

"I shall be so glad when it's over," she said, with a smile, turning from Langley's gaze. "I hate business of every kind."

"You will have no house in town?"

"I shall never live in London again."

Langley threw aside his hat and gloves, stood for a moment with his hands behind him, then looked steadily at her.

"Somewhere on the Continent—wouldn't that be better?"

"No. Fallowfield will be my home."

"You know why I have come to-day?"

Their eyes met. He saw the quivering strain she put upon herself to reply quietly.

"Much better that you hadn't come. But let it be over as soon as possible."

"Your answer is still the same?"

"As I told you it would be."

The sound of hammering came from above. Langley struggled with the frantic impulse of his nerves.

"What are you going to *do* down there?" he asked, with uncivil abruptness.

"Live very quietly, and—and try to atone for all my sins and follies."

Her voice broke midway, but she forced it to complete the sentence.

"I see. In other words, bury yourself alive. Turn ascetic—torment yourself—find merit in misery. And in defiance of the brain that tells you that this is the greatest sin and folly of all! Well, happily it isn't possible."

"The impossible thing," she answered, in a tone of forbearance, "is to make you understand how much I have suffered, and how greatly I have changed."

Her soft, low accents subdued his violence.

"Dearest, how can you so deceive yourself? You—you—to be cloistered, and imagine that your soul will profit by it! You know it is mere illusion. Do good, if you will; and first of all," he smiled, "give yourself to the man whose supreme need is the need of you."

"You have had my answer."

"Only the answer prompted by a mistaken sense of duty. Your duty is to fulfil yourself—to be all it is in your power to be. Yield yourself to a man's love, and be perfect woman."

He held his hands to her; she drew back, and spoke impetuously.

"You mean the woman who has no will of her own? You have my answer, and must accept it."

He gazed at her, as if for a moment doubting; but saw that in her face which roused him to impassioned tenderness.

"How strange it is, Agnes. We seem so far apart. The long years of utter separation—the meeting at length in cold formality—the bitterness, the reproaches—so much that seems to stand between us; and yet we are everything to each other. If you were the kind of woman who has no will of her own, could I love you as I do? And if I were less conscious of my own purpose, would you listen to me? There is no question of one yielding to the other, save in the moment which overcomes your pride and leaves you free to utter the truth. Those are the old phrases of love-making—they rise to a man's tongue when his blood is hot. We shall never see the world with the same eyes: man and woman never did so, never will; but there is no life for us apart from each other. Our very faults make us born companions. Your need of me is as great as mine of you. We have forgiven all there is to forgive; we know what may be asked, and what may not. No castles in the air; no idealisms of boy and girl; but two lives that have a want, and see but the one hope of satisfying it."

He waited, and saw her lips still harden themselves against him.

"You pretend to read my thoughts, yet you have no understanding of my strongest motive. This is quite enough to prove that we are really far apart, and not only seem to be so."

"Then add one word," said Langley. "Say that you don't love me—say it plainly and honestly—and there's an end."

Her self-command was overborne by a rush of tears.

"Why will you torture me? I am trying so hard to do right. My life is misery, and there is only one way to gain peace of mind. I must do as my conscience bids. It is *you* who deceive yourself. What real love can you feel for a woman whom you can't respect? You have said you don't respect me—and how should you? I have lived so basely. Since my marriage, not a day I can look back upon without shame. I am trying to humble myself; to live in the spirit of the religion which I *believe*, though I have so long forgotten it. I hated Mrs. Tresilian, because she seemed to rob me of the love I prized so. It was paltry jealousy—of a piece with all the rest of my life. Now I have forced myself to beg for her good will. I will do all I can to help her—in the way she taught Louis to follow. And you, too, I have injured, in my selfishness. Forgive me, if you can. For me there is no happiness—or only in self denial. I have lived through the worst; I have broken with the world which was everything to me—ambitions, pleasures. Don't make it harder for me. I am doing as you bid me—trying to be all it is in my power to be—all the *good*, after so much evil."

Langley had grasped her hand.

"If you can make me believe that your life will really be better apart from me. I wait for that one word. Do you love me, or not?"

She drew away, but he detained her. The trembling body which at any moment his strength could overcome seemed to declare his victory over the soul. Conventions, social and personal, the multiform restraints upon civilised man before the woman he desires, but who will not yield herself, vanished like a tissue in fire. She was falling, but his arm supported her. So slight and weak a tenement of flesh, now that the proud spirit was exorcised. Holding her, heart to heart, he saw the anguished pallor of her face flush into rosy shame, saw the moist eyes dilate, the lips throb—all of her divinely young and beautiful.

"No—no—I cannot——"

"You can and will——"

"I *cannot* marry you! I have said that I should never marry again, said it so solemnly——"

"To some one else, you mean. What of that! It is *force majeure*." He laughed exultantly.

"I cannot!"

"Not at once. Time to think and understand and accept your dread fate—why, of course. Time even to repent, Agnes, though not in sackcloth and ashes. You have done ill, and so have I, but it is not to be repaired by asceticism. Break down the walls about you—not add to their height and thickness! Walk in the summer sunlight, dearest, and look to the rising of many a summer sun!"

"What right have I to take the easy path?"

"Health and joy are the true repentance. All sins against the conscience—what are they but sins against the law of healthy life?"

"I have sinned so against others. And to make no atonement in my own suffering——"

"The old false thought. Health and joy—it is what life demands of us. And then remember. To marry a mere unheraldic mortal, to exchange the style of chivalry for a bourgeois prefix—is not that punishment enough? I almost fear to ask it of you."

She released herself and stood apart, head dropping.

"I have given no promise. A long time must pass——"

Langley smiled.

XIV

ON an October afternoon Langley sat in his old room at Athens, writing. But no books were piled about him, and his countenance had undergone a change since the day when he bent in idle enjoyment over the page of Aristophanes. It was graver, yet not so old; smoother, but more virile. Play of features—a light in the eye, a motion of brow and lips—expressed the thoughts he was penning.

"Once, when we turned together out of the hot, dusty highroad into a little village graveyard shadowed with cypresses—it was near Colonus, by the banks of the Cephisus—Louis read with pleasure the Greek words painted on the wooden crosses: Ενθάδε κεῖται—classical Greek, looking so strange to him in this modern application. Could it have been done without pedantry, I should have liked to set the words on his marble; to my ear they are better than 'Here lies'; so restful in their antiquity, echoing so softly the music of the old world. But the simplest inscription is the best—the one name by which we called him, and the date of his death. Happily he does not lie among the foolish monstrosities of the Greek cemetery, which I described to you—the skulls and bones, the gilded shirt-studs, and so on. Your wish is respected: on the marble is carved a cross.

"The day has been hot, and in the town intolerably glaring. Soon after sunrise I went to Phaleron and bathed, then lingered about the seashore, thinking—well, of what should I think? You were in your garden, no doubt, among the leaves and flowers of English autumn. I saw you walking there, alone, and hoped that your thoughts were on the shore of Attica.

"Then a midday meal with Worboys. I like the old pedant, and feel for him no little respect. After all, he does what I myself am bent on doing; the business of archæology has taken such strong possession of him that he lives in it with abounding vigour. He has no thought at all for the modern world; to him every interest of to-day—save the doings of excavators—seems vulgar and irrelevant. After all, this is admirable. All the more so that he is utterly devoid of personal ambition; he cares not the least to make a name, and to be respectfully regarded by his fellows. He loves an inscription for its own sake. If he has a personal hope in the matter, I rather think it would take the form of a desire to die in the trenches, and be buried at Colonus along with Ottfried Müller and Charles Lenormant. But he is too humble to express such a wish.

"Heavens! you should hear him talk of you. The Medici had no such incense of laudatory gratitude as Worboys burns daily upon your altar. He sincerely believes that history can show no grander instance of benevolent and enlightened patronage. He will carve your name on the walls of some temple yet unearthed. He will chant you in the valleys of Peloponnesus, and perhaps in the wildernesses of Asia Minor. Now all this is very fine; it tells of a sound heart, and possibly of a brain far from contemptible. Woman in the flesh he will never love (he speaks tenderly of the Caryatides on the Acropolis), but you he worships. I find it inspiriting to be with him. By the by, I have of course told him nothing. About Louis he shall never know more than he does now.

"The day after to-morrow he goes off with his German friend. They are more than brothers. For my own part, I stay here until I have a letter from you. I am impatient, of course. Whatever you write——''

A knock at the door stayed his hand. He bade enter, and there appeared a boy, who, showing white teeth in a smile, and uttering a few words of Greek, delivered a letter.

Alone again, Langley let the unbroken envelope lie before him. He could read the first post-mark, and he observed the date. When his hand was quite steady, he took a penknife and released the sheet of note-paper. It presented but a few lines. After reading them several times, he put the letter in his pocket, hid away his own unfinished writing, and went out.

A few hours later he dined with Worboys and the archæologist's German comrade. It was a cheerful meal, but Langley chose to listen rather than to talk. Afterwards they sat smoking for a long time; then the English friends walked a short distance together.

"It's uncertain, then, how long you stay?" said Worboys.

"No. I have decided to leave to-morrow. And, by the by, I am going back to be married."

Worboys stood still.

"You amaze me!"

"Surely there are more improbable things?"

"Of course, of course. But—you never hinted——. Will you tell me who it is?"

"Yes. You know her. It is Lady Revill."

Worboys drew a deep breath, and clutched his friend's hand.

"I can't say what I should wish to. This is wonderful and magnificent! Ah, what things have happened since we met in the Kerameikos!"

When Langley was in his room again he returned to the unfinished writing.

"I was interrupted by the arrival of your letter. After reading it, I went out and rambled till dark. The sunset was unspeakably glorious—the last of many such that I have seen at Athens. This morning I wished that you were here; at evening, as I stood on the Areopagus, I was glad to know that I had to travel to find you—in the world of realities.

"As Louis said, this is mere fairyland; to us of the north, an escape for rest amid scenes we hardly believe to be real. The Acropolis, rock and ruins all tawny gold, the work of art inseparable from that of nature, and neither seeming to have bodily existence; the gorgeous purples of Hymettus; that cloud on Pentelikon, with its melting splendours which seemed to veil the abode of gods—what part has all this in our actual life? Who cares to know the modern names of these mountains? Who thinks of the people who dwell among them? Worboys is right; living in the past, he forgets the present altogether. I, whose life is now to begin, must shake off this sorcery of Athens, and remember it only as a delightful dream. Mere fairyland; and our Louis has become part of it—to be remembered by me as calmly, yet as tenderly, as this last sunset.

"Dearest, I finish this letter and post it here. It may possibly reach you at Fallowfield a few hours before I come. I have no word of thanks, no word of love that I can *write*. But already I am with you. Yes, let the past be past. To you and me, the day that is still granted us."

THE END